WEST OF THE
TULAROSA

Louis L'Amour

WEST OF THE
TULAROSA

LEISURE BOOKS NEW YORK CITY

A LEISURE BOOK®

July 2010

Published by special arrangement with Golden West Literary Agency.

Dorchester Publishing Co., Inc.
200 Madison Avenue
New York, NY 10016

ISBN 10: 0-8439-6410-3
ISBN 13: 978-0-8439-6410-3
E-ISBN: 978-1-4285-0896-5

The name "Leisure Books" and the stylized "L" with design are trademarks of Dorchester Publishing Co., Inc.

Printed in the United States of America.

10 9 8 7 6 5 4 3 2 1

Visit us online at www.dorchesterpub.com.

CONTENTS

Introduction
by Jon Tuska

Louis Dearborn LaMoore (1908–1988) was born in Jamestown, North Dakota. He left home at fifteen and subsequently held a wide variety of jobs although he worked mostly as a merchant seaman. From his earliest youth, L'Amour had a love of verse. His first published work was a poem, "The Chap Worth While", appearing when he was eighteen years old in his former hometown's newspaper, the *Jamestown Sun*. It is the only poem from his early years that he left out of SMOKE FROM THIS ALTAR, which appeared in 1939 from Lusk Publishers in Oklahoma City, a book which L'Amour published himself; however, this poem is reproduced in THE LOUIS L'AMOUR COMPANION (Andrews and McMeel, 1992) edited by Robert Weinberg. L'Amour wrote poems and articles for a number of small circulation arts magazines all through the early 1930s and, after hundreds of rejection slips, finally had his first story accepted, "Anything for a Pal" in *True Gang Life* (10/35). He returned in 1938 to live with his family where they had settled in Choctaw, Oklahoma, determined to make writing his career. He wrote a fight story bought by Standard Magazines that year and became acquainted with editor Leo Margulies, who was to play an important rôle later in L'Amour's life. "The Town No Guns Could Tame" in *New Western* (3/40) was his first published Western story.

During the Second World War L'Amour was drafted and ultimately served with the U.S. Army Transportation Corps in Europe. However, in the two years before he was shipped out, he managed to write a great many adventure stories for Standard Magazines. The first story he published in 1946, the year of his discharge, was a Western, "Law of the Desert Born" in *Dime Western* (4/46). A talk with Leo Margulies resulted in L'Amour's agreeing to write Western stories for the various Western pulp magazines published by Standard Magazines, a third of which appeared under the byline Jim Mayo, the name of a character in L'Amour's earlier adventure fiction. The proposal for L'Amour to write new Hopalong Cassidy novels came from Margulies, who wanted to launch *Hopalong Cassidy's Western Magazine* to take advantage of the popularity William Boyd's old films and new television series were enjoying with a new generation. Doubleday & Company agreed to publish the pulp novelettes in hard cover books. L'Amour was paid $500 a story, no royalties, and he was assigned the house name Tex Burns. L'Amour read Clarence E. Mulford's books about the Bar-20 and based his Hopalong Cassidy on Mulford's original creation. Only two issues of the magazine appeared before it ceased publication.

Doubleday felt that the Hopalong character had to appear exactly as William Boyd did in the films and on television and thus the novels in book form had to be revamped to meet with this requirement prior to publication.

L'Amour's first Western novel under his own byline was *Westward the Tide* (World's Work, 1950). It was rejected by every American publisher to which it was submitted. World's Work paid a flat £75 without royalties for British Empire rights in perpetuity. L'Amour sold his first Western short story to a slick magazine a year later, "The Gift of Cochise" in *Collier's* (7/5/52). Robert Fellows and John Wayne purchased screen rights to this story from L'Amour for $4,000 and James Edward Grant, one of Wayne's favorite screenwriters, developed a script from it, changing L'Amour's Ches Lane to Hondo Lane. L'Amour retained the right to novelize Grant's screenplay, which differs substantially from his short story, and he was able to get an endorsement from Wayne to be used as a blurb, stating that *Hondo* was the finest Western Wayne had ever read. *Hondo* (Fawcett Gold Medal, 1953) by Louis L'Amour was released on the same day as the film, *Hondo* (Warner, 1953), with a first printing of 320,000 copies.

With *Showdown at Yellow Butte* (Ace, 1953) by Jim Mayo, L'Amour began a series of short Western novels for Don Wollheim that could be doubled with other short novels by other authors in Ace Publishing's paperback two-fers. Advances on these were $800 and usually the author never earned any royalties. *Heller with a Gun* (Fawcett

Gold Medal, 1955) was the first of a series of original Westerns L'Amour had agreed to write under his own name following the success for Fawcett of *Hondo*. L'Amour wanted even this early to have his Western novels published in hard cover editions. He expanded "Guns of the Timberland" by Jim Mayo in *West* (9/50) for *Guns of the Timberlands* (Jason Press, 1955), a hard cover Western for which he was paid an advance of $250. Another novel for Jason Press followed and then *Silver Cañon* (Avalon Books, 1956) for Thomas Bouregy & Company.

The great turn in L'Amour's fortunes came about because of problems Saul David was having with his original paperback Westerns program at Bantam Books. Fred Glidden had been signed to a contract to produce two original paperback Luke Short Western novels a year for an advance of $15,000 each. It was a long-term contract but, in the first ten years of it, Fred only wrote six novels. Literary agent Marguerite Harper then persuaded Bantam that Fred's brother, Jon, could help fulfill the contract and Jon was signed for eight Peter Dawson Western novels. When Jon died suddenly before completing even one book for Bantam, Harper managed to engage a ghost writer at the Disney studios to write these eight "Peter Dawson" novels, beginning with *The Savages* (Bantam, 1959). They proved inferior to anything Jon had ever written and what sales they had seemed to be due only to the Peter Dawson name.

Saul David wanted to know from L'Amour if *he* could deliver two Western novels a year. L'Amour said he could, and he did. In fact, by 1962 this number was increased to three original paperback novels a year. The first L'Amour novel to appear under the Bantam contract was *Radigan* (Bantam, 1958).

Yet I feel that some of Louis L'Amour's finest work is to be found in his early magazine fiction. Several of those stories are collected here, reprinted as they first appeared, and possessing the characteristics in purest form that I suspect account in largest measure for the loyal following Louis L'Amour won from his readers: the young male hero who is in the process of growing into manhood and who is evaluating other human beings and his own experiences; a resourceful frontier woman who has beauty as well as fortitude; and the powerful, romantic, strangely compelling vision of the American West that invests L'Amour's Western fiction and makes it such a delightful escape from the cares of a later time—in this author's words, that "big country needing big men and women to live in it" and where there was no place for "the frightened or the mean."

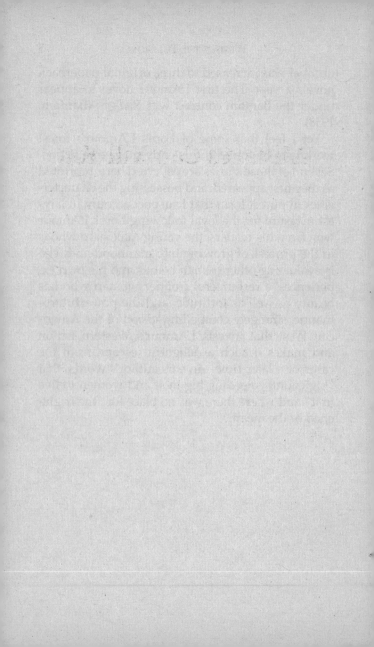

Mistakes Can Kill You

Ma Redlin looked up from the stove. "Where's Sam? He still out yonder?"

Johnny rubbed his palms on his chaps. "He ain't comin' to supper, Ma. He done rode off."

Pa and Else were watching him, and Johnny saw the hard lines of temper around Pa's mouth and eyes. Ma glanced at him apprehensively, but when Pa did not speak, she looked to her cooking. Johnny walked around the table and sat down across from Else.

When Pa reached for the coffeepot, he looked over at Johnny. "Was he alone, boy? Or did he ride off with that no-account Albie Bower?"

It was in Johnny neither to lie nor to carry tales. Reluctantly he replied: "He was with somebody. I reckon I couldn't be sure who it was."

Redlin snorted and put down his cup. It was a sore point with Joe Redlin that his son and only child should take up with the likes of Albie Bower. Back in Pennsylvania and Ohio the Redlins had been good God-fearing folk, while Bower was no good, and came from a no-good outfit. Lately he had been flashing money around, but he claimed to have won it gambling at Degner's Four Star Saloon.

"Once more I'll tell him," Redlin said harshly. "I'll have no son of mine traipsin' with that Four Star outfit. Pack of thieves, that's what they are."

Ma looked up worriedly. She was a buxom woman with a round apple-cheeked face. Good humor was her normal manner. "Don't you be sayin' that away from home, Joe Redlin. That Loss Degner is a gunslinger, and he'd like nothin' so much as to shoot you after you takin' Else from him."

"I ain't afeerd of him." Redlin's voice was flat. Johnny knew that what he said was true. Joe Redlin was not afraid of Degner, but he avoided him, for Redlin was a small rancher, a one-time farmer, and not a fighting man. Loss Degner was bad all through and made no secret of it. His Four Star was the hangout for all the tough element, and Degner had killed two men since Johnny had been in the country, as well as pistol-whipping a half dozen more.

It was not Johnny's place to comment, but secretly he knew the older Redlin was right. Once he had even gone so far as to warn Sam, but it only made the older boy angry.

Sam was almost twenty-one and Johnny but seventeen, but Sam's family had protected him and he had lived always close to the competence of Pa Redlin. Johnny had been doing a man's work since he was thirteen, fighting a man's battles, and making his own way in a hard world.

Johnny also knew what only Else seemed to guess, that it was Hazel, Degner's red-haired singer, who drew Sam Redlin to the Four Star. It was rumored that she was Degner's woman, and Johnny had said as much to Sam. The younger Redlin had flown into a rage and, whirling on Johnny, had drawn back his fist. Something in Johnny's eyes stopped him, and, although Sam would never have admitted it, he was suddenly afraid.

Like Else, Johnny had been adrift when he came to the B Bar. Half dead with pneumonia, he had come up to the door on his black gelding, and the Redlins' hospitality had given him a bed and the best care the frontier could provide, and, when Johnny was well, he went to work to repay them. Then he stayed on for the spring roundup as a forty-a-month hand.

He volunteered no information, and they asked him no questions. He was slightly built and below medium height, but broad-shouldered and wiry. His shock of chestnut hair always needed cutting, and his green eyes held a lurking humor. He moved with deceptive slowness, but he was quick at work, and skillful with his hands. Nor did he wait to be told about things, for even before he began riding, he had mended the buckboard, cleaned out and shored up the spring, repaired the door hinges, and cleaned all the guns.

"We collect from Walters tomorrow," Redlin said suddenly. "Then I'm goin' to make a payment on that Sprague place and put Sam on it. With his own place he'll straighten up and go to work."

Johnny stared at his plate, his appetite gone. He knew what that meant, for it had been in Joe Redlin's mind that Sam should marry Else and settle on that place. Johnny looked up suddenly, and his throat tightened as he looked at her. The gray eyes caught his, searched them for an instant, and then moved away, and Johnny watched the lamplight in her ash blonde hair, turning it to old gold.

He pushed back from the table and excused himself, going out into the moonlit yard. He lived in a room he had built into a corner of the barn. They had objected at first, wanting him to stay at the house, but he could not bear being close to Else, and then he had the lonely man's feeling for seclusion. Actually it had other advantages, for it kept him near his horse, and he never knew when he might want to ride on.

That black gelding and his new .44 Winchester had been the only incongruous notes in his get-up when he arrived at the B Bar, for he had hidden his guns and his best clothes in a cave up the mountain, riding down to the ranch in shabby range clothes with only the .44 Winchester for safety.

He had watched the ranch for several hours despite his illness before venturing down to the door. It paid to be careful, and there were men about who might know him.

Later, when securely in his own room, he had returned to his cache and dug out the guns and brought his outfit down to the ranch. Yet nobody had ever seen him with guns on, nor would they, if he was lucky.

The gelding turned its head and nickered at him, rolling its eyes at him. Johnny walked into the stall and stood there, one hand on the horse's neck.

"Little bit longer, boy, then we'll go. You sit tight now."

There was another reason why he should leave now, for he had learned from Sam that Flitch was in town. Flitch had been on the Gila during the fight, and he had been a friend of Card Wells, who Johnny had killed at Picacho. Moreover, Flitch had been in Cimarron a year before that when Johnny, only fifteen then, had evened the score with the men who had killed his father and stolen their outfit. Johnny had gunned two of them down and put the third into the hospital.

Johnny was already on the range when Sam Redlin rode away the next morning to make his collection. Pa Redlin rode out with Else and found Johnny branding a yearling. Pa waved and rode on, but Else sat on her horse and watched him. "You're a good hand, Johnny," she said when he released the calf. "You should have your own outfit."

"That's what I want most," he admitted. "But I reckon I'll never have it."

"You can if you want it enough. Is it because of what's behind you?"

He looked up quickly then. "What do you know of me?"

"Nothing, Johnny, but what you've told us. But once, when I started into the barn for eggs, you had your shirt off and I saw those bullet scars. I know bullet scars because my own father had them. And you've never told us anything, which usually means there's something you aren't anxious to tell."

"I guess you're right." He tightened the girth on his saddle. "There ain't much to tell, though. I come West with my pa, and he was a lunger. I drove the wagon myself after we left Independence. Clean to Caldwell, then on to Santa Fe. We got us a little outfit with what Pa had left, and some mean fellers stole it off us, and they killed Pa."

Joe Redlin rode back to join them as Johnny was swinging into the saddle. He turned and glanced down at the valley. "Reckon that range won't get much use, Johnny," he said anxiously, "and the stock sure need it. Fair to middlin' grass, but too far to water."

"That draw, now," Johnny suggested. "I've been thinkin' about that draw. It would take a sight of work, but a couple of good men with teams and some elbow grease could build them a dam across that draw. There's a sight of water comes down when it rains, enough to last most of the summer if it was dammed. Maybe even the whole year."

The three horses started walking toward the draw, and Johnny pointed out what he meant. "A feller over to Mobeetie did that one time," he said, "and it washed his dam out twice, but the third time she held, and he had him a little lake, all the year around."

"That's a good idea, Johnny." Redlin studied the set-up and then nodded. "A right good idea."

"Sam and me could do it," Johnny suggested, avoiding Pa Redlin's eyes.

Pa Redlin said nothing, but both Johnny and Else knew that Sam was not exactly ambitious about extra work. He was a good hand, Sam was, strong and capable, but he was big-headed about things and was little inclined to sticking with a job.

"Reminds me," Pa said, glancing at the sun. "Sam should be back soon."

"He might stop in town," Else suggested, and was immediately sorry she had said it for she could see the instant worry on Redlin's face. The idea of Sam Redlin stopping at the Four Star with $7,000 on him was scarcely a pleasant one. Murder had been done there for much, much less. And then Sam was overconfident. He was even cocky.

"I reckon I'd better ride in and meet him," Redlin said, genuinely worried now. "Sam's a good boy, but he sets too much store by himself. He figures he can take care of himself anywhere, but that pack of wolves. . . ." His voice trailed off to silence.

Johnny turned in his saddle. "Why, I could just as well ride in, Pa," he said casually. "I ain't been to town for a spell, and, if anything happened, I could lend a hand."

Pa Redlin was about to refuse, but Else spoke up quickly. "Let him go, Pa. He could do some things for me, too, and Johnny's got a way with folks. Chances are he could get Sam back without trouble."

That's right! Johnny's thoughts were grim. *Send me along to save your boy. You don't care if I get shot, just so's he's been saved. Well, all right, I'll go. When I come back, I'll climb my gelding and light out. Up to Oregon. I've never been to Oregon.*

Flitch was in town. His mouth tightened a little, but at that it would be better than Pa's going. Pa

.

always said the wrong thing, being outspoken like. He was a man who spoke his mind, and to speak one's mind to Flitch or Loss Degner would mean a shooting. It might be he could get Sam out of town all right. If he was drinking, it would be hard. Especially if that redhead had her hands on him.

"You reckon you could handle it?" Pa asked doubtfully.

"Sure," Johnny said, his voice a shade hard, "I can handle it. I doubt if Sam's in any trouble. Later, maybe. All he'd need is somebody to side him."

"Well," Pa was reluctant, "better take your Winchester. My six-gun, too."

"You hang onto it. I'll make out."

Johnny turned the gelding and started back toward the ranch, his eyes cold. Seventeen he might be, but four years on the frontier on your own make pretty much of a man out of you. He didn't want any more shooting, but he had six men dead on his back trail now, not counting Comanches and Kiowas. Six, and he was seventeen. Next thing, they would be comparing him to Billy the Kid or to Wes Hardin.

He wanted no gunfighter's name, only a little spread of his own where he could run a few cows and raise horses, good stock, like some he had seen in east Texas. No range ponies for him, but good blood. That Sprague place now . . . but that was Sam's place, or as good as his. Well, why not? Sam was getting Else, and it was little enough he could do for Pa and Ma, to bring Sam home safe.

He left the gelding at the water trough and

walked into the barn. In his room he dug some saddle gear away from a corner and, out of a hiding place in the corner, he took his guns. After a moment's thought, he took but one of them, leaving the .44 Russian behind. He didn't want to go parading into town with two guns on him, looking like a sure-enough shooter. Besides, with only one gun and the change in him, Flitch might not spot him at all.

Johnny was at the gate, riding out, when Else rode up. Else looked at him, her eyes falling to the gun on his hip. Her face was pale and her eyes large. "Be careful, Johnny. I had to say that because you know how hot-headed Pa is. He'd get killed, and he might get Sam killed."

That was true enough, but Johnny was aggrieved. He looked her in the eyes. "Sure, that's true, but you didn't think of Sam, now, did you? You were just thinking of Pa."

Her lips parted to protest, but then her face seemed to stiffen. "No, Johnny, it wasn't only Pa I thought of. I did think of Sam. Why shouldn't I?"

That was plain enough. Why shouldn't she? Wasn't she going to marry him? Wasn't Sam getting the Sprague place when they got that money back safe?

He touched his horse lightly with a spur and moved on past her. All right, he would send Sam back to her, if he could. It was time he was moving on, anyway.

The gelding liked the feel of the trail and moved out fast. Ten miles was all, and he could do that easy enough, and so he did it, and Johnny turned

the black horse into the street and stopped before
the livery stable, swinging down. Sam's horse
was tied at the Four Star's hitch rail. The saddlebags were gone.

Johnny studied the street, and then crossed it
and walked down along the buildings on the same
side as the Four Star. He turned quickly in to the
door.

Sam Redlin was sitting at a table with the redhead, the saddlebags on the table before him, and
he was drunk. He was very drunk. Johnny's eyes
swept the room. The bartender and Loss Degner
were standing together, talking. Neither of them
paid any attention to Johnny, for neither knew him.
But Flitch did.

Flitch was standing down the bar with Albie
Bower, but none of the old Gila River outfit. Both
of them looked up, and Flitch kept looking, never
taking his eyes from Johnny. Something bothered
him, and maybe it was the one gun.

Johnny moved over to Sam's table. They had to
get out of here fast, before Flitch remembered. "Hi,
Sam," he said. "Just happened to be in town, and
Pa said, if I saw you, to side you on the way home."

Sam stared at him sullenly. "Side me? You?" He
snorted his contempt. "I need no man to side me.
You can tell Pa I'll be home later tonight." He
glanced at the redhead. "Much later."

"Want I should carry this stuff home for you?"
Johnny put his hand on the saddlebags.

"Leave him be," Hazel protested angrily. "Can't
you see he don't want to be bothered? He's capable

of takin' care of himself, an' he don't need no kid for gardeen."

"Beat it," Sam said. "You go on home. I'll come along later."

"Better come now, Sam." Johnny was getting worried, for Loss Degner had started for the table.

"Here, you." Degner was sharp. "Leave that man alone. He's a friend of mine, and I'll have no saddle tramp annoying my customers."

Johnny turned on him. "I'm no saddle tramp. I ride for his pa. He asked me to ride home with him . . . now. That's what I aim to do."

As he spoke, he was not thinking of Degner, but of Flitch. The gunman was behind him now, and neither Flitch, fast as he was, nor Albie Bower was above shooting a man in the back.

"I said to beat it." Sam stared at him drunkenly. "Saddle tramp's what you are. Folks never should have took you in."

"That's it," Degner said. "Now get out. He don't want you nor your company."

There was a movement behind him, and he heard Flitch say: "Loss, let me have him. I know this *hombre*. This is that kid gunfighter, Johnny O'Day, from the Gila."

Johnny turned slowly, his green eyes flat and cold.

"Hello, Flitch. I heard you were around." Carefully he moved away from the table, aware of the startled look on Hazel's face, the suddenly tight awareness on the face of Loss Degner. "You lookin for me, Flitch?" It was a chance he had to take. His best chance now. If shooting started, he might grab the saddlebags and break for the door and then the ranch. They would be through with Sam Redlin once the money was gone.

"Yeah." Flitch stared at him, his unshaven face hard with the lines of evil and shadowed by the intent that rode him hard. "I'm lookin' for you. Always figured you got off easy, made you a fast rep gunnin' down your betters."

Bower had moved up beside him, but Loss Degner had drawn back to one side. Johnny's eyes never left Flitch. "You in this, Loss?"

Degner shrugged. "Why should I be? I was no Gila River gunman. This is your quarrel. Finish it between you."

"All right, Flitch," Johnny said. "You want it. I'm givin' you your chance to start the play."

The stillness of a hot midafternoon lay on the Four Star. A fly buzzed against the dusty, cobwebbed back window. Somewhere in the street a horse stamped restlessly, and a distant pump creaked. Flitch stared at him, his little eyes hard and bright. His sweat-stained shirt was torn at the shoulder, and there was dust ingrained in the pores of his face.

His hands dropped in a flashing draw, but he had only cleared leather when Johnny's first bullet hit him, puncturing the Bull Durham tag that hung from his shirt pocket. The second shot cut the edge of it, and the third, fourth, and fifth slammed into Albie Bower, knocking him back step by step, but Albie's gun was hammering, and it took the sixth shot to put him down.

Johnny stood over them, staring down at their bodies, and then he turned to face Loss Degner.

Degner was smiling, and he held a gun in his hand from which a thin tendril of smoke lifted. Startled, Johnny's eyes flickered to Sam Redlin.

Sam lay across the saddlebags, blood trickling from his temples. He had been shot through the head by Degner under cover of the gun battle, murdered without a chance!

Johnny O'Day's eyes lifted to Loss Degner's. The saloonkeeper was still smiling. "Yes, he's dead, and I've killed him. He had it coming, the fool. Thinking we cared to listen to his bragging. All we wanted was that money, and now we've got it. Me . . . Hazel and I. We've got it."

"Not yet." Johnny's lips were stiff and his heart was cold. He was thinking of Pa, Ma, and Else. "I'm still here."

"You?" Degner laughed. "With an empty gun? I counted your shots, boy. Even Johnny O'Day is cold turkey with an empty gun. Six shots . . . two for Flitch, and beautiful shooting, too, but four shots for Albie, who was moving and shooting, not so easy a target. But now I've got you. With you dead, I'll just say Sam came here without any money, that he got shot during the fight. Sound good to you?"

Johnny still faced him, his gun in his hand. "Not bad," he said, "but you still have me here, Loss. And this gun ain't empty."

Degner's face tightened and then relaxed. "Not empty? I counted the shots, kid, so don't try bluffing me. Now I'm killing you." He tilted his gun toward Johnny O'Day, and Johnny fired once, twice . . . a third time. As each bullet hit him, Loss Degner jerked and twisted, but the shock of the wounds, and death wounds they were, was nothing to the shock of the bullets from that empty gun.

He sagged against the bar and then slipped toward the floor.

Johnny moved in on him. "You can hear me, Loss?" The killer's eyes lifted to his. "This ain't a six-shooter. It's a Watch twelve-shot Navy gun, thirty-six caliber. She's right handy, Loss, and it only goes to show you shouldn't jump to conclusions."

Hazel sat at the table, staring at the dying Degner.

"You better go to him, Red," Johnny said quietly. "He's only got a minute."

She stared at him as he picked up the saddlebags and backed to the door.

Russell, the storekeeper, was on the steps with a half dozen others, none of whom he knew. "Degner killed Sam Redlin," he said. "Take care of Sam, will you?"

At Russell's nod, Johnny swung to the saddle and turned the gelding toward home.

He wouldn't leave now. He couldn't leave now. They would be all alone there, without Sam. Besides, Pa was going to need help on that dam. "Boy," he touched the gelding's neck, "I reckon we got to stick around for a while."

The Man from Battle Flat

At half past four Krag Moran rode in from the cañon trail, and within ten minutes half the town knew that Ryerson's top gun hand was sitting in front of the Palace.

Nobody needed to ask why he was there. It was to be a showdown between Ryerson and the Squaw Creek nesters, and the showdown was to begin with Bush Leason.

The Squaw Creek matter had divided the town, yet there was no division where Bush Leason was concerned. The big nester had brought his trouble on himself, and, if he got what was coming to him, nobody would be sorry. That he had killed five or six men was a known fact.

Krag Moran was a lean, wide-shouldered young man with smoky eyes and a still, Indian-dark face. Some said he had been a Texas Ranger, but all the town knew about him for sure was that he had got back some of Ryerson's horses that had been run off. How he would stack up against a sure-thing killer like Bush Leason was anybody's guess.

Bush Leason was sitting on a cot in his shack when they brought him the news that Moran was in town. Leason was a huge man, thick through the waist and with a wide, flat, cruel face. When they told him, he said nothing at all, just continued to clean his double-barreled shotgun. It was the gun that had killed Shorty Grimes.

Shorty Grimes had ridden for Tim Ryerson, and between them cattleman Ryerson and rancher Chet Lee had sewed up all the range on Battle Flat. Neither of them drifted cattle on Squaw Creek, but for four years they had been cutting hay from its grass-rich meadows, until the nesters had moved in.

Ryerson and Lee ordered them to leave. They replied the land was government land open to filing. Hedrow talked for the nesters, but it was Bush Leason who wanted to talk, and Bush was a troublemaker. Ryerson gave them a week and, when they didn't move, tore down fences and burned a barn or two.

In all of this Shorty Grimes and Krag Moran had no part. They had been repping on Carol Duchin's place at the time. Grimes had ridden into town alone and stopped at the Palace for a drink. Leason started trouble, but the other nesters stopped him. Then Leason turned at the door. "Ryerson gave us a week to leave the country. I'm giving you just thirty minutes to get out of town. Then I come a-shooting."

Shorty Grimes had been ready to leave, but after that he had decided to stay. A half hour later there was a challenging yell from the dark street out front. Grimes put down his glass and started for the door, gun in hand. He had just reached the street door when Bush Leason stepped through the back door and ran forward, three light, quick steps.

Bush Leason stopped then, still unseen. "Shorty," he called softly.

Pistol lowered, unsuspecting, Shorty Grimes had turned, and Bush Leason had emptied both barrels of the shotgun into his chest.

One of the first men into the saloon after the shooting was Dan Riggs, editor of *The Bradshaw Journal*. He knew what this meant, knew it and did not like it, for he was a man who hated violence and felt that no good could come of it. Nor had he any liking for Bush Leason. He had warned the nester leader, Hedrow, about him only a few days before.

Nobody liked the killing but everybody was afraid of Bush. They had all heard Bush make his brags and the way to win was to stay alive.

Now Dan Riggs heard that Krag Moran was in town, and he got up from his desk and took off his eye shade. It was no more than ninety feet from the front of the print shop to the Palace and Dan walked over. He stopped there in front of Krag. Dan was a slender, middle-aged man with thin hands and a quiet face. He said: "Don't do it, son. You mount up and ride home. If you kill Leason, that will just be the beginning."

"There's been a beginning. Leason started it."

"Now, look here . . . ," Riggs protested, but Krag interrupted him.

"You better move," he said in that slow Texas drawl of his. "Leason might show up any time."

"We've got a town here," Riggs replied determinedly. "We've got women and homes and decent folks. We don't want the town shot up and we don't want a lot of drunken killings. If you riders can't behave yourselves, stay away from town. Those farmers have a right to live, and they are good, God-fearing people."

Krag Moran just sat there. "I haven't killed anybody," he said reasonably, his face a little solemn. "I'm just a-sittin' here."

Riggs started to speak, then with a wave of exasperated hands he turned and hurried off. And then he saw Carol Duchin.

Carol Duchin was several things. By inheritance, from her father, she owned a ranch that would make two of Ryerson's. She was twenty-two years old, single, and she knew cattle as well as any man. Chet Lee had proposed to her three times and had been flatly refused three times. She both knew and liked Dan Riggs and his wife, and she often stopped overnight at the Riggs's home when in town. Despite that, she was cattle, all the way.

Dan Riggs went at once to Carol Duchin and spoke his piece. Right away she shook her head. "I won't interfere," she replied. "I knew Shorty Grimes and he was a good man."

"That he was," Riggs agreed sincerely, "I only wish they were all as good. That was a dastardly murder and I mean to say so in the next issue of my paper. But another killing won't help things any, no matter who gets killed."

Carol asked him: "Have you talked to Bush Leason?"

Riggs nodded. "He won't listen, either. I tried to get him to ride over to Flagg until things cooled off a little. He laughed at me."

She eyed him curiously.

"What do you want me to do?"

"Talk to Krag. For you, he'll leave."

"I scarcely know him." Carol Duchin was not planning to tell anyone how much she did know about Krag Moran, nor how interested in the tall rider she had become. During his period of repping with her roundup he had not spoken three words to her, but she had noticed him, watched him, and listened to her riders talk about him among themselves.

"Talk to him. He respects you. All of them do."

Yes, Carol reflected bitterly, *he probably does. And he probably never thinks of me as a woman*.

She should have known better. She was the sort of girl no man could ever think of in any other way. Her figure was superb, and she very narrowly escaped genuine beauty. Only her very coolness and her position as owner had kept more than one cowhand from speaking to her. So far only Chet Lee had found the courage. But Chet never lacked for that.

She walked across the street toward the Palace, her heart pounding, her mouth suddenly dry. Now that she was going to speak to Krag, face-to-face, she was suddenly frightened as a child. He got to his feet as she came up to him. She was tall for a girl, but he was still taller. His mouth was firm, his jaw strong and clean-boned. She met his eyes and found them smoky green and her heart fluttered.

"Krag"—her voice was natural at least—"don't stay here. You'll either be killed or you'll kill Bush. In either case it will be just one more step and will just lead to more killing."

His voice sounded amused, yet respectful, too. "You've been talking to Dan Riggs. He's an old woman."

"No"—suddenly she was sure of herself—"no, he's telling the truth, Krag. Those people have a right to that grass, and this isn't just a feud between you and Leason. It means good men are going to be killed, homes destroyed, crops ruined, and the work of months wiped out. You can't do this thing."

"You want me to quit?" He was incredulous. "You know this country. I couldn't live in it, nor anywhere the story traveled."

She looked straight into his eyes. "It often takes a braver man not to fight."

He thought about that, his smoky eyes growing somber. Then he nodded. "I never gave it any thought," he said seriously, "but I reckon you're right. Only I'm not that brave."

"Listen to Dan," she pleaded. "He's an intelligent man. He's an editor. His newspaper means something in this country and will mean more. What he says is important."

"Him?" Krag chuckled. "Why, ma'am, that little varmint's just a-fussin'. He don't mean nothing, and nobody pays much attention to him. He's just a little man with ink on his fingers."

"You don't understand," Carol protested.

* * *

Bush Leason was across the street. During the time Krag Moran had been seated in front of the Palace, Bush had been doing considerable serious thinking. How good Krag was, Bush had no idea, nor did he intend to find out; yet a showdown was coming, and from Krag's lack of action he evidently intended for Bush to force the issue.

Bush was not hesitant to begin it, but the more he considered the situation the less he liked it. The wall of the Palace was stone, so he could not shoot through it. There was no chance to approach Krag from right or left without being seen for some time before his shotgun would be within range. Krag had chosen his position well, and the only approach was from behind the building across the street.

This building was empty, and Bush had gotten inside and was lying there, watching the street when the girl came up. Instantly he perceived his advantage. As the girl left, Krag's eyes would involuntarily follow her. In that instant he would step from the door and shoot Krag down. It was simple and it was foolproof.

"You'd better go, ma'am," Krag said. "It ain't safe here. I'm staying right where I am until Leason shows."

She dropped her hands helplessly and turned away from him. In that instant, Bush Leason stepped from the door across the street and jerked his shotgun to his shoulder. As he did so, he yelled.

Carol Duchin was too close. Krag shoved her

hard with his left hand and stepped quickly right,
drawing as he stepped and firing as his right foot
touched the walk.

Afterward, men who saw it said there had never
been anything like it before. Leason whipped up
his shotgun and yelled, and in the incredibly brief
instant, as the butt settled against Leason's shoulder, Krag pushed the girl, stepped away from her,
and drew. And he fired as his gun came level.

It was split-second timing and the fastest draw
that anybody had ever seen in Bradshaw; the .45
slug slammed into Bush Leason's chest just as he
squeezed off his shot, and the buckshot whapped
through the air, only beginning to scatter at least a
foot and a half over Krag Moran's head. And Krag
stood there, flat-footed, and shot Bush again as he
stood leaning back against the building. The big
man turned sideways and fell into the dust off the
edge of the walk.

As suddenly as that it was done. And then Carol
Duchin got to her feet, her face and clothes dusty.
She brushed her clothes with quick, impatient
hands, and then turned sharply and looked at Krag
Moran. "I never want to see you again!" she flared.
"Don't put a foot on my place! Not for any reason
whatever!"

Krag Moran looked after her helplessly, took
an involuntary step after her, and then stopped. He
glanced once at the body of Bush Leason and the
men gathered around it. Then he walked to his
horse. Dan Riggs was standing there, his face shadowed with worry. "You've played hell," he said.

"What about Grimes?"

"I know, I know. Bush was vicious. He deserved killing, and, if ever I saw murder, it was his killing of Grimes, but that doesn't change this. He had friends, and all of the nesters will be sore. They'll never let it alone."

"Then they'll be mighty foolish." Krag swung into the saddle, staring gloomily at Carol Duchin. "Why did she get mad?"

He headed out of town. He had no regrets about the killing. Leason was a type of man that Krag had met before, and they kept on killing and making trouble until somebody shot too fast for them. Yet he found himself upset by the worries of Riggs as well as the attitude of Carol Duchin. Why was she so angry? What was the matter with everybody?

Moran had the usual dislike for nesters possessed by all cattlemen, yet Riggs had interposed an element of doubt, and he studied it as he rode back to the ranch. Maybe the nesters had an argument, at that. This idea was surprising to him, and he shied away from it.

As the days passed and the tension grew, he found himself more and more turning to thoughts of Carol. The memory of her face when she came across the street toward him and when she pleaded with him, and then her flashing and angry eyes when she got up out of the dust.

No use thinking about her, Moran decided. Even had she not been angry at him, what could a girl who owned the cattle she owned want with a drifting cowhand like himself? Yet he did think about her. He thought about her too much. And then the whole Bradshaw country exploded with a bang. Chet Lee's riders, with several hotheads from the Ryerson outfit, hit the nesters and hit them hard. They ran off several head of cattle, burned haystacks and two barns, killed one man, and shot up several houses. One child was cut by flying glass. And the following morning a special edition of *The Bradshaw Journal* appeared.

ARMED MURDERERS RAID
SLEEPING VALLEY

Blazing barns, ruined crops, and death remained behind last night after another vicious, criminal raid by the murderers, masquerading as cattlemen, who raided the peaceful, sleeping settlement on Squaw Creek.

Ephraim Hershman, 52 years old, was shot down in defense of his home by gunmen from the Chet Lee and Ryerson ranches when they raided Squaw Valley last night. Two other men were wounded, while young Billy Hedrow, 3 years old, was severely cut by flying glass when the night riders shot out the windows. . . .

Dan Riggs was angry and it showed all the way through the news and in the editorial adjoining. In a scathing attack he named names and bitterly assailed the ranchers for their tactics, demanding intervention by the territorial governor.

Ryerson came stamping out to the bunkhouse, his eyes hard and angry. "Come on!" he yelled. "We're going in and show that durned printer where he gets off. Come on! Mount up!"

Chet Lee was just arriving in town when the cavalcade from the Ryerson place hit the outskirts of Bradshaw. It was broad daylight, but the streets of the town were empty and deserted.

Chet Lee was thirty-five, tough as a boot, and with skin like a sun-baked hide. His eyes were cruel, his lips thin and ugly. He shoved Riggs aside and his men went into the print shop, wrecked the hand press, threw the type out into the street, and smashed all the windows out of the shop. Nobody made a move to harm Dan Riggs, who stood pale and quiet at one side. He said nothing to any of them until the end, and then it was to Ryerson.

"What good do you think this will do?" he asked quietly. "You can't stop people from thinking. You can't throttle the truth. In the end it always comes out. Grimes and Leason were shot in fights, but that last night was wanton murder and destruction of property."

"Oh, shut up!" Ryerson flared. "You're getting off lucky."

Lee's little eyes brightened suddenly. "Maybe," he said, "a rope is what this feller needs!"

Dan Riggs looked at Lee without shifting an inch. "It would be like you to think of that," he said, and Lee struck him across the mouth.

Riggs got slowly to his feet, blood running down his lips. "You're fools," he said quietly. "You don't seem to realize that, if you can destroy the property of others, they can destroy it for you. Or do you realize that when any freedom is destroyed for others, it is destroyed for you, too? You've wrecked my shop, ruined my press. Tyrants and bullies have always tried that sort of thing, especially when they are in the wrong."

Nobody said anything. Ryerson's face was white and stiff, and Krag felt suddenly uneasy. Riggs might be a fool but he had courage. It had been a rotten thing for Chet Lee to hit him when he couldn't fight back.

"We fought for the right of a free press and free speech back in 'Seventy-Six," Dan Riggs persisted. "Now you would try to destroy the free press because it prints the truth about you. I tell you now, you'll not succeed."

They left him standing there among the ruins of his printing shop and all he owned in the world, and then they walked to the Palace for a drink. Ryerson waved them to the bar.

"Drinks are on me!" he said. "Drink up!"

Krag Moran edged around the crowd and stopped at Ryerson's elbow. "Got my money, boss?" he asked quietly. "I've had enough."

Ryerson's eyes hardened. "What kind of talk is that?"

Chet Lee had turned his head and was staring hard at Moran. "Don't be a fool."

"I'm not a fool. I'm quitting. I want my money. I'll have no part in that sort of thing this morning. It was a mean, low trick."

"You pointing any part of that remark at me?" Lee turned carefully, his flat, wicked eyes on Krag. "I want to know."

"I'm not hunting trouble." Krag spoke flatly. "I spoke my piece. You owe me forty bucks, Ryerson."

Ryerson dug his hand into his pocket and slapped two gold eagles on the bar. "That pays you off. Now get out of the country. I want no part of turncoats. If you're around here after twenty-four hours, I'll hunt you down like a dog."

Krag had turned away. Now he smiled faintly. "Why, sure. I reckon you would. Well, for your information, Ryerson, I'll be here."

Before they could reply, he strode from the room. Chet Lee stared after him. "I never had no use for that saddle tramp, anyway."

Ryerson bit the end off his cigar. His anger was cooling and he was disturbed. Krag was a solid man. Despite Lee, he knew that. Suddenly he was disturbed—or had it been ever since he saw Dan Riggs's white, strained face? Gloomily he stared down at his whiskey. What was wrong with him? Was he getting old? He glanced at the harsh face of Chet Lee—why wasn't he as sure of himself as Lee? Weren't they here first? Hadn't they cut hay in the valley for four years? What right had the nesters to move in on them?

Krag Moran walked outside and shoved his hat back on his head. Slowly he built a smoke. Why, he was a damned fool! He had put himself right in the middle by quitting. Now he would be fair game for Leason's friends, with nobody to stand beside him. Well, that would not be new. He had stood alone before he came here, and he could again.

He looked down the street. Dan Riggs was squatted in the street, picking up his type. Slowly Krag drew on his cigarette, then he took it from his lips and snapped it into the gutter. Riggs looked up as his shadow fell across him. His face was still dark with bitterness.

Krag nodded at it. "Can you make that thing work again? The press, I mean."

Riggs stared at the wrecked machine. "I doubt it," he said quietly. "It was all I had, too. They think nothing of wrecking a man's life."

Krag squatted beside him and picked up a piece of the type and carefully wiped off the sand. "You made a mistake," he said quietly. "You should have had a gun on your desk."

"Would that have stopped them?"

"No."

"Then I'm glad I didn't have it. Although"—there was a flicker of ironic humor in his eyes—"sometimes I don't feel peaceful. There was a time this afternoon when if I'd had a gun. . . ."

Krag chuckled. "Yeah," he said, "I see what you mean. Now let's get this stuff picked up. If we can get that press started, we'll do a better job . . . and this time I'll be standing beside you."

Two days later the paper hit the street, and copies of it swiftly covered the country.

BIG RANCHERS WRECK JOURNAL PRESS
Efforts of the big ranchers of the Squaw Creek Valley range to stifle the free press have proved futile. . . .

There followed the complete story of the wrecking of the press and the threats to Dan Riggs. Following that was a rehash of the two raids on the nesters, the accounts of the killings of Grimes and Leason, and the warning to the state at large that a full-scale cattle war was in the making unless steps were taken to prevent it.

Krag Moran walked across the street to the saloon, and the bartender shook his head at him. "You've played hob," he said. "They'll lynch both of you now."

"No, they wont. Make mine rye."

The bartender shook his head. "No deal. The boss says no selling to you or Riggs."

Krag Moran's smile was not pleasant. "Don't make any mistakes, Pat," he said quietly. "Riggs might take that. I won't. You set that bottle out here on the bar or I'm going back after it. And don't reach for that shotgun. If you do, I'll part your hair with a bullet."

The bartender hesitated, and then reached carefully for the bottle. "It ain't me, Krag," he objected. "It's the boss."

"Then you tell the boss to tell me." Krag poured a drink, tossed it off, and walked from the saloon.

When Moran crossed the street, there was a sorrel mare tied in front of the shop. He glanced at the brand and felt his mouth go dry. He pushed open the door and saw her standing there in the half shadow—and Dan Riggs was gone.

"He needed coffee," Carol said quietly. "I told him I'd stay until you came back."

He looked at her and felt something moving deep within him, an old feeling that he had known only in the lonesome hours when he had found himself wanting someone, something—and this was it.

"I'm back." She still stood there. "But I don't want you to go."

She started to speak, and then they heard the rattle of hoofs in the street and suddenly he turned and watched the sweeping band of riders come up the street and stop before the shop. Chet Lee was there, and he had a rope.

Krag Moran glanced at Carol. "Better get out of here," he said. "This will be rough." And then he stepped outside.

They were surprised and looked it. Krag stood there with his thumbs hooked in his belt, his eyes running over them. "Hi," he said easily. "You boys figure on using that rope?"

"We figure on hanging an editor," Ryerson said harshly.

Krag's eyes rested on the old man for an instant. "Ryerson," he said evenly, "you keep out of this. I have an idea, if Chet wasn't egging you on, you'd not be in this. I've also an idea that all this trouble centers around one man, and that man is Chet Lee."

Lee sat his horse with his eyes studying Krag carefully. "And what of it?" he asked.

Riggs came back across the street. In his hand he held a borrowed rifle, and his very manner of holding it proved he knew nothing about handling it. As he stepped out in front of the cattlemen, Carol Duchin stepped from the print shop. "As long as you're picking on unarmed men and helpless children," she said clearly, "you might as well fight a woman, too."

Lee was shocked. "Carol! What are you doin' here? You're cattle!"

"That's right, Chet. I run some cows. I'm also a woman. I know what a home means to a woman. I know what it meant to Missus Hershman to lose her husband. I'm standing beside Riggs and Moran in this . . . all the way."

"Carol!" Lee protested angrily. "Get out of there! This is man's work! I won't have it!"

"She does what she wants to, Chet," Krag said, "but you're going to fight me."

Chet Lee's eyes came back to Krag Moran. Suddenly he saw it there, plain as day. This man had done what he had failed to do; he had won. It all boiled down to Moran. If he was out of the way. . . .

"Boss"—it was one of Ryerson's men—"look out."

Ryerson turned his head. Three men from the nester outfit stood ranged at even spaces across the street. Two of them held shotguns, one a Spencer rifle. "There's six more of us on the roofs!" Hedrow called down. "Anytime you want to start your play, Krag, just open the ball."

Ryerson shifted in his saddle. He was suddenly sweating, and Krag Moran could see it. Nevertheless, Moran's attention centered itself on Chet Lee. The younger man's face showed his irritation and his rage at the futility of his position. Stopped by the presence of Carol, he was now trapped by the presence of the nesters.

"There'll be another day!" He was coldly furious. "This isn't the end!"

Krag Moran looked at him carefully. He knew all he needed to know about the man he faced. Chet Lee was a man driven by a passion for power. Now it was the nesters, later it would be Ryerson, and then, unless she married him, Carol Duchin. He could not be one among many; he could not be one of two. He had to stand alone.

"You're mistaken, Chet," Moran said. "It ends here."

Chet Lee's eyes swung back to Krag. For the first time he seemed to see him clearly. A slow minute passed before he spoke. "So that's the way it is?" he said softly.

"That's the way it is. Right now you can offer your holdings to Ryerson. I know he has the money to buy them. Or you can sell out to Carol, if she's interested. But you sell out, Chet. You're the troublemaker here. With you gone, I think Ryerson and Hedrow could talk out a sensible deal."

"I'll talk," Hedrow said quietly, "and I'll listen."

Ryerson nodded. "That's good for me. And I'll buy, Chet. Name a price."

Chet Lee sat perfectly still. "So that's the way it is?" he repeated. "And if I don't figure to sell?"

"Then we take your gun and start you out of town," Krag said quietly.

Lee nodded. "Yeah, I see. You and Ryerson must have had this all figured out. A nice way to do me out of my ranch. And your quitting was all a fake."

"There was no plan," Moran said calmly. "You've heard what we have to say. Make your price. You've got ten minutes to close a deal or ride out without a dime."

Chet Lee's face did not alter its expression. "I see," he said. "But suppose something happens to you, Krag? Then what? Who here could make me toe the line? Or gamble I'd not come back?"

"Nothing's going to happen to me." Krag spoke quietly. "You see, Chet, I know your kind."

"Well"—Chet shrugged, glancing around—"I guess you've got me." He looked at Ryerson. "Fifty thousand?"

"There's not that much in town. I'll give you twelve, and that's just ten thousand more than you hit town with."

"Guess I've no choice," Chet said. "I'll take it." He looked at Krag. "All right if we go to the bank?"

"All right."

Chet swung his horse to the right, but, as he swung the horse, he suddenly slammed his right spur into the gelding's ribs. The bay sprang sharply left, smashing into Riggs and knocking him down. Only Krag's quick leap backwards against the print shop saved him from going down, too. As he slammed home his spur, Chet grabbed for his gun. It came up fast and he threw a quick shot that splashed Krag Moran's face with splinters, then he swung his horse and shot, almost point-blank, into Krag's face.

But Moran was moving as the horse swung, and, as the horse swung left, Moran moved away. The second shot blasted past his face and then his own guns came up and he fired two quick shots. So close was Chet Lee that Krag heard the slap of the bullets as they thudded into his ribs below the heart.

Lee lost hold of his gun and slid from the saddle, and the horse, springing away, narrowly missed stepping on his face.

Krag Moran stood over him, looking down. Riggs was climbing shakily to his feet, and Chet was alive yet, staring at Krag.

"I told you I knew your kind, Chet," Krag said quietly. "You shouldn't have tried it."

Carol Duchin was in the café when Krag Moran crossed the street. He had two drinks under his belt and he was feeling them, which was rare for him. Yet he hadn't eaten and he could not remember when he had.

She looked up when he came through the door and smiled at him. "Come over and sit down," she said. "Where's Dan?"

Krag smiled with hard amusement. "Getting money from Ryerson to buy him a new printing outfit."

"Hedrow?"

"Him and the nesters signed a contract to supply Ryerson with hay. They'd have made a deal in the beginning if it hadn't been for Chet. Hedrow tried to talk business once before. I heard him."

"And you?"

He placed his hat carefully on the hook and sat down. He was suddenly tired. He ran his fingers through his crisp, dark hair. "Me?" He blinked his eyes and reached for the coffeepot. "I'm going to shave and take a bath. Then I'm going to sleep for twenty hours about, and then I'm going to throw the leather on my horse and hit the trail."

"I told you over there," Carol said quietly, "that I didn't want you to go."

"Uhn-uh. If I don't go now"—he looked at her somberly—"I'd never want to go again."

"Then don't go," she said.

And he didn't.

The Lion Hunter
and the Lady

The mountain lion stared down at him with wild, implacable eyes and snarled deep in its chest. He was big, one of the biggest Morgan had seen in his four years of hunting them. The lion crouched on a thick limb not over eight feet above his head.

"Watch him, Cat," Lone John Williams warned. "He's the biggest I ever seen. The biggest in these mountains, I'll bet."

"You ever seen Lop-Ear?" Morgan queried, watching the lion. "He's half again bigger than this one." He jumped as he spoke, caught a limb in his left hand, and then swung himself up as easily as a trapeze performer.

The lion came to its feet then and crouched, growling wickedly, threatening the climbing man. But Morgan continued to mount toward the lion.

"Give me that pole!" Morgan called to the older man. "I'll have this baby in another minute!"

"You watch it," Williams warned. "That lion ain't foolin'."

Never in the year he had been working with Cat Morgan had Lone John become accustomed to seeing a man go up a tree after a mountain lion. Yet in that period Morgan had captured more than fifty lions alive and had killed as many more. Morgan was not a big man as big men are counted, but he was tall, lithe, and extraordinarily strong. Agile as a cat, he climbed trees, cliffs, and rocky slopes after the big cats, for which he was named, and had made a good thing out of supplying zoo and circus animal buyers.

With a noose at the end of the pole, and only seven feet below the snarling beast, Morgan lifted the pole with great care. The lion struck viciously and then struck again, and in that instant after the second strike, Morgan put the loop around his neck and drew the noose tight. Instantly the cat became a snarling, clawing, spitting fury, but Morgan swung down from the tree, dragging the beast after him.

Before the yapping dogs could close with him, Lone John tossed his own loop, snaring the lion's hind legs. Morgan closed with the animal, got a loop around the powerful forelegs, and drew it tight. In a matter of seconds the mountain lion was neatly trussed and muzzled, with a stick thrust into its jaws between its teeth, and its jaws tied shut with rawhide.

Morgan drew a heavy sack around the animal and then tied it at the neck, leaving the lion's head outside.

Straightening, Cat Morgan took out the makings and began to roll a smoke. "Well," he said, as he put the cigarette between his lips, "that's one more and one less."

Hard-ridden horses sounded in the woods and then a half dozen riders burst from the woods and a yell rent the air. "Got 'em, Dave! Don't move, you!" The guns the men held backed up their argument, and Cat Morgan relaxed slowly, his eyes straying from one face to another, finally settling on the big man who rode last from out of the trees.

This man was not tall, but blocky and powerful. His neck was thick and his jaw wide. He was clean-shaven, unusual in this land of beards and mustaches. His face wore a smile of unconcealed satisfaction now, and, swinging down, he strode toward them. "So, you finally got caught, didn't you? Now how smart do you feel?"

"Who do you think we are?" Morgan asked coolly. "I never saw you before."

"I reckon not, but we trailed you right here. You've stole your last horse. Shake out a loop, boys. We'll string 'em up right here."

"Be careful with that talk," Lone John said. "We ain't horse thieves an' ain't been out of the hills in more'n a year. You've got the wrong men."

"That's tough," the big man said harshly, "because you hang, here and now."

"Maybe they ain't the men, Dorfman. After all, we lost the trail back yonder a couple of miles." The speaker was a slender man with black eyes and swarthy face.

Without turning, Dorfman said sharply: "Shut up! When I want advice from a 'breed, I'll ask it."

His hard eyes spotted the burlap sack. The back of it lay toward him, and the lion's head was faced away from him. All he saw was the lump of the filled sack. "What's this? Grub?" He kicked hard at the sack, and from it came a snarl of fury.

Dorfman jumped and staggered back, his face white with shock. Somebody laughed, and Dorfman wheeled, glaring around for the offender. An old man with gray hair and a keen, hard face looked at Morgan. "What's in that sack?" he demanded.

"A mountain lion," Cat replied calmly. "A nice, big, live lion. Make a good pet for your loud-mouthed friend." He paused and then smiled tolerantly at Dorfman. "If he wouldn't be scared of him."

Dorfman's face was livid. Furious that he had been frightened before these men, and enraged at Morgan as the cause of it, he sprang at Morgan and swung back a huge fist. Instantly Cat Morgan stepped inside the punch, catching it on an upraised forearm. At the same instant he whipped a wicked right uppercut to Dorfman's wind. The big man gasped and paled. He looked up, and Morgan stepped in and hooked hard to the body, and then the chin. Dorfman hit the ground in a lump.

Showing no sign of exertion, Morgan stepped back. He looked at the older man. "He asked for it," he said calmly. "I didn't mind, though." He glanced at Dorfman, who was regaining his breath and his senses, and then his eyes swung back to the older man. "I'm Cat Morgan, a lion hunter. This is Lone John Williams, my partner. What Lone John said was true. We haven't been out of the hills in a year."

"He's telling the truth." It was the half-breed.

The man was standing beside the tree. "His hounds are tied right back here, an' from the look of this tree they just caught that cat. The wood is still wet where the bark was skimmed from the tree by his boots."

"All right, Loop." The older man's eyes came back to Morgan. "Sorry. Reckon we went off half-cocked. I've heard of you."

A wiry, yellow-haired cowhand leaned on his pommel. "You go up a tree for the cats?" he asked incredulously. "I wouldn't do it for a thousand dollars!"

Dorfman was on his feet. His lips were split and there was a cut on his cheek bone. One eye was rapidly swelling. He glared at Morgan. "I'll kill you for this!" he snarled.

Morgan looked at him. "I reckon you'll try," he said. "There ain't much man in you, just brute and beef."

The older man spoke up quickly. "Let's go, Dorf. This ain't catchin' our thief."

As the cavalcade straggled from the clearing, the man called Loop loitered behind. "Watch yourself, Morgan," he said quietly. "He's bad, that Dorfman. He'll never rest until he kills you, now. He won't take it lyin' down."

"Thanks." Cat's gray-green eyes studied the half-breed. "What was stolen?"

Loop jerked his head. "Some of Dorfman's horses. Blooded stock, stallion, three mares, and four colts."

Morgan watched him go, and then walked back down the trail for the pack animals. When they had the cat loaded, Lone John left him to take it back to camp.

Mounting his own zebra dun, Morgan now headed downcountry to prospect a new cañon for cat sign. He had promised a dealer six lions and he had four of them. With luck he could get the other two this week. Only one of the hounds was with him, a big, ugly brute that was one of the two best lion dogs he had, just a mongrel. Big Jeb was shrewd beyond average. He weighed one hundred and twenty pounds and was tawny as the lions he chased.

The plateau was pine-clad, a thick growth that spilled over into the deep cañon beyond, and that cañon was a wicked jumble of wrecked ledges and broken rock. At the bottom he could hear the roar and tumble of a plunging mountain stream, although he had never seen it. That cañon should be home for a lot of lions.

There was no trail. The three of them—man, dog, and horse—sought a trail down, working their way along the rim over a thick cover of pine needles. At last Cat Morgan saw the slope fall away steeply, but at such a grade that he could walk the horse to the bottom. Slipping occasionally on the needles, they headed down.

Twice Jeb started to whine as he picked up old lion smell, but each time he was dissuaded by Cat's sharp-spoken command.

There was plenty of sign. In such a cañon as this it should take him no time at all to get his cats. He was walking his horse and rolling a smoke when he heard the sound of an axe. It brought him up, standing.

It was impossible! There could be nobody in this wild area, nobody! Not in all the days they had worked the region had they seen more than one or two men until they encountered the horse-thief hunters.

Carefully he went on, calling Jeb close to the horse and moving on with infinite care. Whoever was in this wilderness would be somebody he would want to see before he was seen. He remembered the horse thieves whose trail had been lost. Who else could it be?

Instantly he saw evidence of the correctness of his guess. In the dust at the mouth of the cañon were tracks of a small herd of horses.

Grimly he eased his Colt in the holster. Horse thieves were a common enemy, and, although he had no liking for Dorfman, this was his job, too.

Taller than most, Cat Morgan was slender of waist. Today he wore boots, but usually moccasins. His red flannel shirt was sun-faded and patched, his black jeans were saddle polished, and his face was brown from sun and wind, hollow-cheeked under the keen gray-green eyes. His old hat was black and flat-crowned. It showed rough usage.

Certainly the thief had chosen well. Nobody would ever find him back in here. The horses had turned off to the right. Following, Cat went down, through more tumbled rock and boulders, and then drew up on the edge of a clearing.

It was after sundown here. The shadows were

long, but near the far wall was the black oblong of a cabin, and light streamed through a window and the wide-open door.

Dishes rattled, the sound of a spoon scraping something from a dish, and he heard a voice singing. A woman's voice.

Amazed, he started walking his horse nearer, yet the horse had taken no more than a step when he heard a shrill scream, a cry odd and inhuman, a cry that brought him up short. At the same instant, the light in the house went out and all was silent. Softly he spoke to his horse and walked on toward the house.

He heard the click of a back-drawn hammer, and a cool girl's voice said: "Stand right where you are, mister! And if you want to get a bullet through your belt buckle, just start something!"

"I'm not moving," Morgan said impatiently. "But this isn't a nice way to greet visitors."

"Who invited you?" she retorted. "What do you want, anyway? Who are you?"

"Cat Morgan. I'm a lion hunter. As for being invited, I've been a lot of places without being invited. Let me talk to your dad or your husband."

"You'll talk to me. Lead your horse and start walking straight ahead. My eyes are mighty good, so if you want to get shot, just try me."

With extreme care, Morgan walked on toward the house. When he was within a dozen paces, a shrill but harsh voice cried: "Stand where you are! Drop your guns!"

Impatiently Morgan replied: "I'll stand where I

am, but I won't drop my guns. Light up and let's see who you are."

Someone moved, and later there was a light. Then the girl spoke. "Come in, you."

She held a double-barreled shotgun and she was well back inside the door. A tall, slender but well-shaped girl, she had rusty red hair and a few scattered freckles. She wore a buckskin shirt that failed to conceal the lines of her lovely figure.

Her inspection of him was cool, careful. Then she looked at the big dog that had come in and stood alongside him. "Lion hunter? You the one who has that pack of hounds I hear nearby every day?"

He nodded. "I've been running lions up on the plateau. Catching 'em, too."

She stared. "Catching them? Alive? Sounds to me like you have more nerve than sense. What do you want live lions for?"

"Sell 'em to some circus or zoo. They bring anywhere from three to seven hundred dollars, depending on size and sex. That beats punching cows."

She nodded. "It sure does, but I reckon punching cows is a lot safer."

"How about you?" he said. "What's a girl doing up in a place like this? I didn't have any idea there was anybody back in here."

"Nor has anybody else up to now. You won't tell, will you? If you go out of here and tell, I'll be in trouble. Dorfman would be down here after me in a minute."

"For stealing horses?" Morgan asked shrewdly.

Her eyes flashed. "They are not his horses. They are mine. Every last one of them." She lowered the gun a trifle. "Dorfman is both a bully and a thief. He stole my dad's ranch, then his horses. That stallion is mine, and so are the mares and their get."

"Tell me about it," he suggested. Carefully he removed his hat.

She studied him doubtfully, and then lowered the gun. "I was just putting supper on. Draw up a chair."

"Let's eat!" a sharp voice yelled. Startled, Cat looked around and for the first time saw the parrot in the cage.

"That's Pancho," she explained. "He's a lot of company. I'm Laurie Madison."

Her father had been a trader among the Nez Percé Indians, and from them he obtained the splendid Appaloosa stallion and the mares from which his herd was started. When Karl Dorfman appeared, there had been trouble. Later, while she was East on a trip, her father had been killed by a fall from a horse. Returning, she found the ranch sold and the horses gone.

"They told me the stallion had thrown him. I knew better. It had been Dorfman and his partner, Ad Vetter, who found Dad. And then they brought bills against the estate and forced a quick sale of all property to satisfy them. The judge worked with them. Shortly after, the judge left and bought a ranch of his own. Dad never owed money to anyone. I believe they murdered him."

"That would be hard to prove. Did you have any evidence?"

"Only what the doctor said. He told me the blows could not have been made by the fall. He believed Dad had been struck while lying on the ground."

Cat Morgan believed her. Whether his own dislike of Dorfman influenced it, he did not know. Somehow the story rang true. He studied the problem thoughtfully. "Did you get anything from the ranch?"

"Five hundred dollars and a ticket back East." Anger flashed in her eyes as she leaned toward him to refill his cup. "Mister Morgan, that ranch was worth at least forty thousand dollars. Dad had been offered that much and refused it."

"So you followed them?"

"Yes. I appeared to accept the situation, but discovered where Dorfman had gone and followed him, determined to get the horses back, at least."

It was easier, he discovered two hours later, to ride to the secret valley than to escape from it. After several false starts, he succeeded in finding the spot where the lion had been captured that day, and then hit the trail for camp. As he rode, the memory of Dorfman kept returning—a brutal, hard man, accustomed to doing as he chose. He had not seen the last of him, he knew.

Coming into the trees near the camp, Cat Morgan grew increasingly worried, for he smelled no smoke and saw no fire. Speaking to the horse, he rode into the basin and drew up sharply. Before him, suspended from a tree, was a long black burden!

Clapping the spurs to the horse, he crossed the

clearing and grabbed the hanging figure. Grabbing his hunting knife, he slashed the rope that hung him from the tree, and then lowered the old man to the ground. Loosening his clothes, he held his hand over the old man's heart. Lone John was alive!

Swiftly Morgan built a fire and got water. The old man had not only been hanged, but had been shot twice through the body and once through the hand. But he was still alive.

The old man's lids fluttered, and he whispered: "Dorfman. Five of 'em. Hung me . . . heard somethin' . . . they done . . . took off." He breathed hoarsely for a bit. "Figured it . . . it was you . . . reckon."

"*Shhh.* Take it easy now, John. You'll be all right."

"No. I'm done for. That rope . . . I grabbed it . . . held my weight till I plumb give out."

The wiry old hand gripping his own suddenly eased its grip, and the old man was dead.

Grimly Cat got to his feet. Carefully he packed what gear had not been destroyed. The cats had been tied off a few yards from the camp and had not been found. He scattered meat to them, put water within their reach, and returned to his horse. A moment only, he hesitated. His eyes wide-open to what lay ahead, he lifted the old man across the saddle of a horse, and then mounted his own. The trail he took led to Seven Pines.

It was the gray hour before the dawn when he rode into the town. Up the street was the sheriff's office. He knocked a long time before there was a reply. Then a hard-faced man with blue and cold eyes opened the door. "What's the matter? What's up?"

"My partner's been murdered. Shot down, then hung."

"Hung?" The sheriff stared at him, no friendly light in his eyes. "Who hung him?"

"Dorfman. There were five in the outfit."

The sheriff's face altered perceptibly at the name. He walked out and untied the old man's body, lowering it to the stoop before the office. He scowled. "I reckon," he said dryly, "if Dorfman done it, he had good reason. You better light out if you want to stay in one piece."

Unbelieving, Morgan stared at him. "You're the sheriff?" he demanded. "I'm charging Dorfman with murder. I want him arrested."

"You want?" The sheriff glared. "Who the devil are you? If Dorfman hung this man, he had good reason. He's lost horses. I reckon he figured this *hombre* was one of the thieves. Now you slope it afore I lock you up."

Cat Morgan drew back three steps, his eyes on the sheriff. "I see. Lock me up, eh? Sheriff, you'd have a mighty hard job locking me up. What did you say your name was?"

"Vetter, if it makes any difference."

"Vetter, eh? Ad Vetter?" Morgan was watching the sheriff like a cat.

Sheriff Vetter looked at him sharply. "Yes, Ad Vetter. What about it?"

Cat Morgan took another step back toward his horses, his eyes cold now. "Ad Vetter . . . a familiar name in the Nez Percé country."

Vetter started as if struck. "What do you mean by that?"

Morgan smiled. "Don't you know," he said, chancing a long shot, "that you and Dorfman are wanted up there for murdering old man Madison?"

"You're a liar!" Sheriff Vetter's face was white as death. He drew back suddenly, and Morgan could almost see the thought in the man's mind and knew that his accusation had marked him for death. "If Dorfman finds you here, he'll hang you, too."

Cat Morgan backed away slowly, watching Vetter. The town was coming awake now, and he wracked his brain for a solution to the problem. Obviously Dorfman was a man with influence here, and Ad Vetter was sheriff. Whatever Morgan did or claimed was sure to put him in the wrong. And then he remembered the half-breed, Loop, and the older man who had cautioned Dorfman the previous afternoon.

A man was sweeping the steps before the saloon, and Morgan stopped beside him. "Know a man named Loop? A 'breed?"

"Sure do." The sweeper straightened and measured Morgan. "Huntin' him?"

"Yeah, and another *hombre*. Older feller, gray hair, pleasant face but frosty eyes. The kind that could be mighty bad if pushed too hard. I think I heard him called Dave."

"That'll be Allen. Dave Allen. He owns the D over A, west of town. Loop lives right on the edge of town in a shack. He can show you where Dave lives."

Turning abruptly, Morgan swung into the saddle and started out of town. As he rounded the curve toward the bridge, he glanced back. Sheriff Vetter was talking to the sweeper. Cat reflected grimly that it would do him but little good, for unless he had talked with Dorfman the previous night, and he did not seem to have, he would not understand Morgan's reason for visiting the old rancher. And Cat knew that he might be wasting his time.

He recognized Loop's shack by the horse in the corral and drew up before it. The half-breed appeared in the door, wiping an ear with a towel. He was surprised when he saw Cat Morgan, but he listened as Morgan told him quickly about the hanging of Lone John Williams and Vetter's remarks.

"No need to ride after Allen," Loop said. "He's comin' down the road now. Him and Tex Norris. They was due in town this mornin'."

At Loop's hail, the two riders turned abruptly toward the cabin. Dave Allen listened in silence while Cat repeated his story, only now he told all, not that he had seen the girl or knew where she was, but that he had learned why the horses were stolen, and then about the strange death of old man Madison. Dave Allen sat his horse in silence and listened. Tex spat once, but made no other comment until the end. "That's Dorfman, boss. I never did cotton to him."

"Wait." Allen's eyes rested thoughtfully on Cat. "Why tell me? What do you want me to do?"

Cat Morgan smiled suddenly, and, when Tex saw

that smile, he found himself pleased that it was Dorfman this man wanted and not him. "Why, Allen, I don't want you to do anything. Only, I'm not an outlaw. I don't aim to become one for a no-account like Dorfman, nor another like this here Vetter. You're a big man hereabouts, so I figured to tell you my story and let you see my side of this before the trouble starts."

"You aim to go after him?"

Morgan shook his head. "I'm a stranger here, Allen. He's named me for a horse thief, and the law's against me, too. I aim to let them come to me, right in the middle of town."

Loop walked back into his cabin, and, when he came out, he had a Spencer .56, and, mounting, he fell in beside Morgan. "You'll get a fair break," he said quietly, his eyes cold and steady. "I aim to see it. No man who wasn't all right would come out like that and state his case. Besides, you know that old man Williams struck me like a mighty fine old gent."

Dorfman was standing on the steps as they rode up. One eye was barely open, the other swollen. The marks of the beating were upon him. That he had been talking to Vetter was obvious by his manner, although the sheriff was nowhere in sight. Several hardcase cowhands loitered about, the presence creating no puzzle to Cat Morgan.

Karl Dorfman glared at Allen. "You're keepin' strange company, Dave."

The old man's eyes chilled. "You aimin' to tell me who I should travel with, Dorfman? If you are, save your breath. We're goin' to settle more than one thing here today."

"You sidin' with this here horse thief?" Dorfman demanded.

"I'm sidin' nobody. Last night you hanged a man. You're going to produce evidence here today as to why you believed him guilty. If that evidence isn't good, you'll be tried for murder."

Dorfman's face turned ugly. "Why, you old fool. You can't get away with that. Vetter's sheriff, not you. Besides," he sneered, "you've only got one man with you."

"Two," Loop said quietly. "I'm sidin' Allen ... and Cat Morgan, too."

Hatred blazed in Dorfman's eyes. "I never seen no good come out of a 'breed yet!" he flared. "You'll answer for this!"

Dave Allen dismounted, keeping his horse between himself and Dorfman. By that time a good-size crowd had gathered about. Tex Norris wore his gun well to the front, and he kept his eyes roving from one to the other of Dorfman's riders. Cat Morgan watched but said nothing.

Four men had accompanied Dorfman, but there were others here who appeared to belong to his group. With Allen and himself there were only Tex and Loop, and yet, looking at them, he felt suddenly happy. There were no better men than these, Tex with his boyish smile and careful eyes, Loop with his long, serious face. These men would stick. He stepped then into the van, seeing Vetter approach.

Outside their own circle were the townspeople.

These, in the last analysis, would be the judges, and now they were saying nothing. Beside him he felt a gentle pressure against his leg and, looking down, saw Jeb standing there. The big dog had never left him. Morgan's heart was suddenly warm and his mind was cool and ready.

"Dorfman!" His voice rang in the street. "Last night you hung my riding partner. Hung him for a horse thief, without evidence or reason. I charge you with murder. The trail you had followed you lost, as Dave Allen and Loop will testify. Then you took it upon yourself to hang an old man simply because he happened to be in the vicinity."

His voice was loud in the street, and not a person in the crowd but could hear every syllable. Dorfman shifted his feet, his face ugly with anger, yet worried, too. Why didn't Vetter stop him? Arrest him?

"Moreover, the horses you were searching for were stolen by you from Laurie Madison, in Montana. They were taken from the ranch after that ranch had been illegally sold, and after you and Vetter had murdered her father."

"That's a lie!" Dorfman shouted. He was frightened now. There was no telling how far such talk might carry. Once branded, a man would have a lot of explaining to do.

Suppose what Morgan had told Vetter was true? That they were wanted in Montana? Suppose something had been uncovered?

He looked beyond Morgan at Allen, Loop, and Tex. They worried him, for he knew their breed.

Dave Allen was an Indian fighter, known and respected. Tex had killed a rustler only a few months ago in a gun battle. Loop was cool, careful, and a dead shot.

"That's a lie," he repeated. "Madison owed me money. I had papers ag'in' him."

"Forged papers. We're reopening the case, Dorfman, and this time there won't be any fixed judge to side you."

Dorfman felt trapped. Twice Cat Morgan had refused to draw when he had named him a liar, but Dorfman knew it was simply because he had not yet had his say. Of many things he was uncertain, but of one he was positive. Cat Morgan was not yellow.

Before he spoke again, Sheriff Ad Vetter suddenly walked into sight. "I been investigatin' your claim," he said to Morgan, "and she won't hold water. The evidence shows you strung up the old man yourself."

· Cat Morgan shrugged. "Figured something like that from you, Vetter. What evidence?"

"Nobody else been near the place. That story about a gal is all cock and bull. You had some idea of an alibi when you dragged that in here."

"Why would he murder his partner?" Allen asked quietly. "That ain't sense, Ad."

"They got four lions up there. Them lions are worth money. He wanted it all for himself."

Cat Morgan smiled, and, slowly lifting his left hand, he tilted his hat slightly. "Vetter," he said, "you've got a lot to learn. Lone John was my partner only in the camping and riding. He was working for me. I catch my own cats. I've got a contract with Lone John. Got my copy here in my pocket. He's going to be a hard man to replace because he'd learned how to handle cats. I went up the trees after 'em. Lone John was mighty slick with a rope, and, when a lion hit ground, he dropped a rope on 'em fast. I liked that old man, Sheriff, and I'm charging Dorfman with murder like I said. I want him put in jail . . . now!"

Vetter's face darkened. "You givin' orders?"

"If you've got any more evidence against Morgan," Allen interrupted, "trot it out. Remember, I rode with Dorfman on that first posse. I know how he felt about this. He was frettin' to hang somebody, and the beatin' he took didn't set well. He figured Lone John's hangin' would scare Morgan out of the country."

Vetter hesitated, glancing almost apologetically at Dorfman. "Come on, Dorf," he said. "We'll clear you. Come along."

An instant only the rancher hesitated, his eyes ugly. His glance went from Allen back to Cat Morgan, and then he turned abruptly. The two men walked away together. Dave Allen looked worried and he turned to Morgan. "You'd better get some evidence, Cat," he said. "No jury would hang him on this, or even hold him for trial."

It was late evening in the cabin and Laurie filled Cat's cup once more. Outside, the chained big cats prowled restlessly, for Morgan had brought them down to the girl's valley to take better care of them, much to the disgust of Pancho, who stared at them from his perch and scolded wickedly.

"What do you think will happen?" Laurie asked. "Will they come to trial?"

"Not they, just Dorfman. Yes, I've got enough now so that I can prove a fair case against him. I've found a man who will testify that he saw him leave town with four riders and head for the hills, and that was after Allen and that crowd had returned. I've checked that rope they used, and it is Dorfman's. He used a hair rope, and 'most everybody around here uses rawhide reatas. Several folks will swear to that rope."

"Horse thief," Pancho said huskily. "Durned horse thief."

"Be still," Laurie said, turning on the parrot. "You be still!"

Jeb lifted his heavy head and stared curiously, his head cocked at the parrot that looked upon Jeb with almost as much disfavor as the cats.

"These witnesses are all afraid of Dorfman, but, if he is brought to trial, they will testify."

Suddenly Pancho screamed, and Laurie came to her feet, her face pale. From the door there was a dry chuckle. "Don't scream, lady. It's too late for that." It was Ad Vetter's voice.

Cat Morgan sat very still. His back was toward the door, his eyes on Laurie's face. He was thinking desperately.

"Looks like this is the showdown." That was Dorfman's voice. He stepped through the door and shoved the girl. She stumbled back and sat down hard on her chair. "You little fool! You wouldn't take that ticket and money and let well enough alone. You had to butt into trouble. Now you'll die for it, and so will this lion-huntin' friend of yours."

The night was very still. Jeb lay on the floor, his head flattened on his paws, his eyes watching Dorfman. Neither man had seemed to notice the parrot. "Allen will be asking why you let Dorfman out," Morgan suggested, keeping his voice calm.

"He don't know it," Vetter said smugly. "Dorf'll be back in jail afore mornin', and in a few days, when you don't show up as a witness against him, he'll he freed. Your witnesses won't talk unless you get Dorf on trial. They're scared. As for Dave Allen, we'll handle him later, and that 'breed, too."

"Too bad it won't work," Morgan said. Yet even as he spoke, he thought desperately that this was the end. He didn't have a chance. Nobody knew of this place, and the two of them could be murdered here, buried, and probably it would be years before the valley was found. Yet it was Laurie of whom he was thinking now. It would be nothing so easy as murder for her, not to begin with. And knowing the kind of men Dorfman and Vetter were, he could imagine few things worse for any girl than to be left to their mercy.

He made up his mind then. There was no use waiting. No use at all. They would be killed; the time to act was now. He might get one or both of them before they got him. As it was, he was doing nothing, helping none at all.

"You two," he said, "will find yourselves looking through cottonwood leaves at the end of a rope."

"Horse thief!" Pancho screamed. "Durned horse thief!"

Both men wheeled, startled by the unexpected voice, and Cat left his chair with a lunge. His big shoulder caught Dorfman in the small of the back and knocked him sprawling against the pile of wood beside the stove. Vetter whirled and fired as he turned, but the shot missed, and Morgan caught him with a glancing swing that knocked him sprawling against the far wall. Cat Morgan went after him with a lunge, just as Dorfman scrambled from the wood pile and grabbed for a gun. He heard a fierce growl and whirled just as Jeb hurtled through the air, big jaws agape.

The gun blasted, but the shot was high and Jeb seized the arm in his huge jaws, and then man and dog went rolling over and over on the floor. Vetter threw Morgan off and came to his feet, but Morgan lashed out with a left that knocked him back through the door. Dorfman managed to get away from the dog and sprang through the door just as Ad Vetter came to his feet, grabbing for his gun.

Cat Morgan skidded to a stop, realizing even as his gun flashed up that he was outlined against the lighted door. He felt the gun buck in his hand, heard the thud of Vetter's bullet in the wall beside him, and saw Ad Vetter turn half around and fall on his face. At the same moment a hoarse scream rang out behind the house, and, darting around, Morgan saw a dark figure rolling over and over on the ground among the chained lions!

Grabbing a whip, he sprang among them, and in the space of a couple of breaths had driven the lions back. Then he caught Dorfman and dragged him free of the beasts. Apparently blinded by the sudden rush from light into darkness, and mad to escape from Jeb, the rancher had rushed right into the middle of the lions. Laurie bent over Morgan. "Is . . . is he dead?"

"No. Get some water on, fast. He's living, but he's badly bitten and clawed." Picking up the wounded man, he carried him into the house and placed him on the bed.

Quickly he cut away the torn coat and shirt. Dorfman was unconscious but moaning.

"I'd better go for the doctor," he said.

"There's somebody coming now, Cat. Riders."

Catching up his rifle, Morgan turned to the door. Then he saw Dave Allen, Tex, and Loop with a half dozen other riders. One of the men in a dark coat was bending over the body of Ad Vetter.

"The man who needs you is in here," Morgan said. "Dorfman ran into my lions in the dark."

Dave Allen came to the door. "This clears you, Morgan," he said, "and I reckon a full investigation will get this lady back her ranch, or what money's left, anyway. And full title to her horses. Loop," he added, "was suspicious. He watched Vetter and saw him slip out with Dorfman, and then got us and we followed them. They stumbled onto your trail here, and we came right after, but we laid back to see what they had in mind."

"Thanks." Cat Morgan glanced over at Laurie, and their eyes met. She moved quickly to him. "I reckon, Allen, we'll file a claim on this valley. Both of us are sort of attached to it."

"Don't blame you. Nice place to build a home."

"That," Morgan agreed, "is what I've been thinking."

The One for the
Mohave Kid

We had finished our antelope steak and beans, and the coffeepot was back on the stove again, brewing strong, black cowpuncher coffee just like you'd make over a creosote and ironwood fire out on the range.

Red Temple was cleaning his carbine and Doc Lander had tipped back in his chair with a pipe lighted. The stove was cherry red, the woodbox full, and our beds were warming up for the night. It was early autumn, but the nights were already cool. In a holster, hanging from the end of a bunk, was a worn-handled, single-action .44 pistol—and the holster had seen service as well as the gun.

"Whenever," Doc Lander said, "a bad man is born, there is also born a man to take him. For every Billy the Kid there is a Pat Garrett, an' for every Wes Hardin there's a John Selman."

Red picked up a piece of pinewood, and, flicking open the stove door, he chucked it in. He followed it with another, and we all sat silent, watching the warm red glow of the flames. When the door was shut again, Red looked up from his rifle. "An' for every John Selman there's a Scarborough," he said, "an' for every Scarborough, a Logan."

"Exactly," Doc Lander agreed, "an' for every Mohave Kid there's a. . . ."

Some men are born to evil, and such a one was the Mohave Kid. Now I'm not saying that environment doesn't have its influence, but some men are born with twisted minds, just as some are born with crooked teeth. The Mohave Kid was born with a streak of viciousness and cruelty that no kindness could eradicate. He had begun to show it when a child, and it developed fast until the Kid had killed his first man.

It was pure, unadulterated murder. No question of fair play, although the Kid was deadly with any kind of a gun. He shot an old Mexican, stole his outfit and three horses that he sold near the border. And the Mohave Kid was fifteen years old when that happened.

By the time he was twenty-two he was wanted in four states and three territories. He had, the records said, killed eleven men. Around the saloons and livery stables they said he had killed twenty-one. Actually he had killed twenty-nine, for the Kid had killed a few when they didn't know he was in the country, and they had been listed as murders by Indians or travelers. Of the twenty-nine men he had killed, nine of them had been killed with something like an even break.

But the Mohave Kid was as elusive as he was treacherous. And his mother had been a Holdstock. There were nine families of Holdstocks scattered through Texas, New Mexico, and Arizona, and three times that many who were kinfolk. They were a clannish lot, given to protecting their own, even as bad an apple as the Mohave Kid.

At twenty-two, the Kid was five feet seven inches tall and weighed one hundred and seventy pounds. He had a round, flat face, a bland expression, and heavy-lidded eyes. He did not look alert, but his expression belied the truth, for he was always wary, always keyed for trouble.

He killed for money, for horses, in quarrels, or for pure cruelty, and several of his killings were as senseless as they were ruthless. This very fact contributed much to the fear with which he was regarded, for there was no guessing where he might strike next. People avoided looking at him, avoided even the appearance of talking about him when he was around. Usually they got out of a place when he came into it, but as unobtrusively as possible.

Aside from the United States Marshals or the Texas Rangers in their respective bailiwicks, there was only local law. Little attention was given to arresting men for crimes committed elsewhere, which served as excuse for officers of the law who preferred to avoid the risks of trying to arrest the Mohave Kid.

Ab Kale was an exception. Ab was thirty-three when elected marshal of the cow town of Hinkley, and he owned a little spread of his own three miles out of town. He ran a few cows, raised a few horses, and made his living as marshal. For seven years he was a good one. He kept order, never made needless arrests, and was well liked around town.

At thirty-four he married Amie Holdstock, a second cousin to the Mohave Kid.

As the Kid's reputation grew, Kale let it be known throughout the family that he would make no exception of the Kid, and the Kid was to stay away from Hinkley. Some of the clan agreed this was fair enough, and the Kid received word to avoid the town. Others took exception to Kale's refusal to abide by clan law where the Kid was concerned, but those few dwindled rapidly as the Kid's murderous propensities became obvious.

The Holdstock clan began to realize that in the case of the Mohave Kid they had sheltered a viper in their bosom, a wanton killer as dangerous to their well-being as to others. A few doors of the clan were closed against him, excuses were found for not giving him shelter, and the feeling began to permeate the clan that the idea was a good one.

The Mohave Kid had seemed to take no exception to the hints that he avoid making trouble for cousin Kale, yet as the months wore on, he became more sullen and morose, and the memory of Ab Kale preyed upon his mind.

In the meantime, no man is marshal of a Western cow town without having some trouble. Steady and considerate as Kale was, there had been those with whom he could not reason. He had killed three men.

All were killed in fair, stand-up gunfights, all were shot cleanly and surely, and it was talked around that Kale was some hand with a gun himself. In each case he had allowed an even break and proved faster than the men he killed. All of this the Mohave Kid absorbed, and here and there he heard speculation, never in front of him, that the Mohave Kid was avoiding Hinkley because he wanted no part of Ab Kale.

Tall, well-built, and prematurely gray, Kale was a fine-appearing man. His home was small but comfortable, and he had two daughters, one his own child, one a stepdaughter of seventeen named Ruth who he loved as his own. He had no son, and this was a matter of regret.

Ab Kale was forty when he had his showdown with the Mohave Kid. But on the day when Riley McClean dropped off a freight train on the edge of Hinkley, the date of that showdown was still two years away.

If McClean ever told Kale what had happened to him before he crawled out of that empty boxcar in Hinkley, Ab never repeated it. Riley was nineteen, six feet tall, and lean as a rail. His clothes were in bad shape, and he was unshaven and badly used up, and somebody had given him a beating. What had happened to the other fellow or fellows, nobody ever knew.

Ab Kale saw McClean leave the train and called out to him. The boy stopped and stood, waiting. As Kale walked toward him, he saw the lines of hunger in the boy's face, saw the emaciated body, the ragged clothes, the bruises and cuts. He saw a boy who had been roughly used, but there was still courage in his eyes.

"Where you headed for, son?"

Riley McClean shrugged. "This is as good a place as any. I'm hunting a job."

"What do you do?"

" 'Most anything. It don't make no difference."

Now when a man says that he can do almost anything, it is a safe bet he can do nothing, or at least that he can do nothing well. If a man has a trade, he is proud of it and says so, and usually he will do a passing job of anything else he tackles. Yet Kale reserved his opinion. And it was well that he did.

"Better come over to my office," Kale said. "You'll need to get shaved and washed up."

McClean went along, and somehow he stayed. Nothing was ever said about leaving by either of them. McClean cleaned up, ate at the marshal's expense, and then slept the clock around. When Kale returned to the office and jail the next morning, he found the place swept, mopped, and dusted, and McClean was sitting on the cot in the open cell where he had slept, repairing a broken reata.

Obviously new to the West, Riley McClean seemed new to nothing else. He had slim, graceful hands and deft fingers. He cobbled shoes, repaired harnesses, built a chimney for Chalfant's new house, and generally kept busy,

After he had been two weeks in Hinkley, Ab Kale was sitting at his desk one day when Riley McClean entered. Kale opened a drawer and took out a pair of beautifully matched .44 Russians, one of the finest guns Smith & Wesson ever made. They were thrust in new holsters on a new belt studded with cartridges. "If you're going to live out here, you'd better learn to use those," Kale said briefly.

After that the two rode out of town every morning for weeks, and in a narrow cañon on the back of Kale's little ranch Riley McClean learned how to use a six-shooter.

"Just stand naturally," Kale advised him, "and let your hand swing naturally to the gun butt. You've probably heard about a so-called gunman's crouch. There is no such thing among gunfighters who know their business. Stand any way that is easy to you. Crouching may make a smaller target of you, but it also puts a man off balance and cramps his movements. Balance is as important to a gunfighter as to a boxer. Stand easy on your feet, let your hand swing back naturally, and take the hammer spur with the inside of the thumb, cocking the gun as it is grasped, the tip of the trigger finger on the trigger."

Kale watched McClean try it. "The most important thing is a good grip. The finger on the trigger helps to align your gun properly, and, after you've practiced, you'll see that your gun will line up perfectly with that grip."

He watched McClean keenly and was pleased. The boy had the same ease with a gun he seemed to have with all tools, and his coordination was natural and easy. "You'll find," he added, "in shooting from the hip that you can change your point of aim by a slight movement of your left foot. Practice until you find just the right position for your feet, and then go through the motions until it's second nature."

Finally he left him alone to practice, tossing him a box of shells occasionally. But no day passed that Riley McClean did not take to the hills for practice.

There are men who are born to skill, whose co-ordination of hand, foot, and eye is natural and easy, who acquire skills almost as soon as they lift a tool or a weapon, and such a man was Riley Mc-Clean. Yet he knew the value of persistence, and he practiced consistently.

It was natural that he knew about the Mohave Kid. Riley McClean listened and learned. He talked it around and made friends, and he soon began to hear the speculations about the Kid and Ab Kale.

"It'll come," they all said. "It can't miss. Sooner or later him an' Kale will tangle."

As to what would happen then, there was much dispute. Of this talk Kale said nothing. When Riley McClean had been two months in Hinkley, Kale invited him home to dinner for the first time. It was an occasion to be remembered.

The two months had made a change in Riley. The marks of his beating had soon left him, but it had taken these weeks to fill out his frame. He had gained fifteen solid pounds and would gain more, but he was a rugged young man, bronzed and straight, when he walked up the gravel path to the door of the Kale home. And Ruth Kale opened the door for him. She opened the door and she fell in love. And the feeling was mutual.

Ab Kale said nothing, but he smiled behind his white mustache. Later, when they had walked back up to town, Kale said: "Riley, you've been like a son to me. If anything should happen to me, I wish you would see that my family gets along all right."

Riley was startled and worried. "Nothing will happen to you," he protested. "You're a young man yet."

"No," Kale replied seriously, "I'm not. I'm an old man as a cow town peace officer. I've lasted a long time. Longer than most."

"But you're chain lightning with a gun," Riley protested.

"I'm fast," Kale said simply. "And I shoot straight. I know of no man I'd be afraid to meet face-to-face, although I know some who are faster than I. But they don't always meet you face-to-face."

And Riley McClean knew that Ab Kale was thinking of the Mohave Kid. He realized then, for the first time, that the marshal was worried about the Mohave Kid. Worried because he knew the kind of killer the Kid was. Deadly enough face-to-face, the Kid would be just as likely to shoot from ambush. For the Kid was a killing machine, utterly devoid of moral sense or fair play.

The people of Hinkley knew that Riley McClean had taken to carrying a gun. They looked upon this tolerantly, believing that Riley was merely copying his adopted father. They knew that Kale had been teaching him to shoot, but they had no idea what had happened during those lessons. Nor had Ab Kale realized it until a few days before the pay-off.

The two were riding out to look over some cattle, and Kale remarked that it would be nice to have some rabbit stew. "If we see a fat cottontail," he said, "we'll kill it."

A mile farther along, Kale spotted one. "Rabbit!" he said, and grabbed for his gun.

His hand slapped the walnut butt, and then there was an explosion, and for an instant he thought his own gun had gone off accidentally. And then he saw the smoking .44 in Riley McClean's hand, and the younger man was riding over to pick up the rabbit. The distance had been thirty yards and the rabbit had lost a head.

Ab Kale was startled. He said nothing, however, and they rode on to the ranch, looked over the cattle, and made a deal to buy them. As they started back, Kale commented: "That was a nice shot, Riley. Could you do it again?"

"Yes, sir, I think so."

A few miles farther, another rabbit sprang up. The .44 barked and the rabbit died, half his head and one ear blasted away. The distance was a shade greater than before.

"You've nothing to worry about, Riley," Kale said quietly, "but never use that gun unless you must, and never draw it unless you mean to kill."

Nothing more was said, but Ab Kale remembered. He was fast. He knew he was fast. He knew that he rated along with the best, and yet his hand had barely slapped the butt before that rabbit died. . . .

The days went by slowly, and Riley McClean spent more and more time at the Kale home. And around town he made friends. He was quiet, friendly, and had a healthy sense of humor. He had progressed from the town handyman to opening a shop as a gunsmith, learning his trade by applying it that way. There was no other gunsmith within two hundred miles in any direction, so business was good.

He was working on the firing pin of a Walker Colt when he heard the door open. He did not look up, just said: "Be with you in a minute. What's your trouble?"

"Same thing you're workin' on I reckon. Busted firin' pin."

Riley McClean looked up into a dark, flat face and flat, black eyes. He thought he had never seen eyes so devoid of expression, never seen a face more brutal on a young man. With a shock of realization he knew he was looking into the eyes of the Mohave Kid.

He got to his feet and picked up the gun the Kid handed him. As he picked it up, he noticed that the Kid had his hand on his other gun. Riley merely glanced at him, and then examined the weapon. The repair job was simple, but, as he turned the gun in his hand, he thought of how many men it had killed.

"Take a while," he said. "I s'pose you're in a hurry for it?"

"You guessed it. An' be sure it's done right. I'll want to try it before I pay for it."

Riley McClean's eyes chilled a little. There were butterflies in his stomach, but the hackles on the back of his neck were rising. "You'll pay me before you get it," he said quietly. "My work is cash on the barrel head. The job will be done right." His eyes met the flat black ones. "If you don't like the job, you can bring it back."

For an instant, their eyes held, and then the Kid shrugged, smiling a little. "Fair enough. An' if it doesn't work, I'll be back."

The Mohave Kid turned and walked out to the street, stopping to look both ways. Riley McClean held the gun in his hands and watched him. He felt cold, chilled.

Ab Kale had told the Kid to stay away from Hinkley, and now he must meet him and order him from town. He must do that, or the Kid would know he was afraid, would deliberately stay in town. The very fact that the Mohave Kid had come to Hinkley was proof that he had come hunting trouble, that he had come to call Kale's bluff.

For a minute or two, Riley considered warning the marshal, but that would not help. Kale would hear of it soon enough, and there was always a chance that the Kid would get his gun, change his mind, and leave before Kale did know.

Sitting down, Riley went to work on the gun. The notion of doctoring the gun so it would not fire properly crossed his mind, but there was no use inviting trouble. Running his fingers through his dark rusty hair, he went to work. And as he worked, an idea came to him.

Maybe he could get the Kid out of town to try the gun and, once there, warn him away from Hinkley himself. That would mean a fight, and, while he had no idea of being as good as the Kid, he did know he could shoot straight. He might kill the Mohave Kid even if he got killed in the process.

But he did not want to die. He was no hero, Riley McClean told himself. He wanted to live, buy a place of his own, and marry Ruth. In fact, they had talked about it. And there was a chance this would all blow over. The Kid might leave town before Ab Kale heard of his arrival, or something might happen. It is human to hope and human to wish for the unexpected good break—and sometimes you are lucky.

As Riley was finishing work on the gun, Ruth came in. She was frightened. "Riley"—she caught his arm—"the Mohave Kid's in town and Dad is looking for him."

"I know." He stared anxiously out the window. "The Kid left his gun to be repaired. I've just finished it."

"Oh, Riley, isn't there something we can do?" Her face was white and strained, her eyes large.

He looked down at her, a wave of tenderness sweeping over him. "I don't know, honey," he said gently. "I'm afraid the thing I might do, your father wouldn't like. You see, this is his job. If he doesn't meet the Kid and order him to leave, he will never have the same prestige here again. Everybody knows the Kid came here on purpose."

Ab Kale had heard that the Mohave Kid was in town, and in his own mind he was ready. Seated at his desk, he saw with bitter clarity what he had known all along, that sooner or later the Kid would come to town, and then he would have to kill him or leave the country. There could be no other choice where the Kid was concerned.

Yet he had planned well. Riley McClean was a good man, a steady man. He would make a good husband for Ruth, and together they would see that Amie lacked for nothing. As far as that went, Amie was well provided for. He checked his guns and got to his feet. As he did so, he saw a rider go by, racing out of town.

He stopped dead still in the doorway. Why, that rider had been Riley McClean! Where would he be going at that speed, at this hour? Or had he heard the Kid was in town . . . ? Oh, no! The boy wasn't a coward. Ab knew he wasn't a coward.

He straightened his hat and touched his prematurely white mustache. His eyes studied the street. A few loafers in front of the livery stable, a couple more at the general store, a half dozen horses at the hitch rails. One buckboard. He stepped out on the walk and started slowly up the street. The Mohave Kid would be in the Trail Driver Saloon.

He walked slowly, with his usual measured step. One of the loafers in front of the store got to his feet and ducked into the saloon. All right, then. The Kid knew he was coming. If he came out in the street to meet him, so much the better.

Ruth came suddenly from Riley's shop and started toward him. He frowned and glanced at her. No sign of the Kid yet. He must get her off the street at once.

"Hello, Dad." Her face was strained, but she smiled brightly. "What's the hurry?"

"Don't stop me now, Ruth," he said. "I've got business up the street."

"Nothing that won't wait," she protested. "Come in the store. I want to ask you about something."

"Not now, Ruth." There was still no sign of the Kid. "Not now."

"Oh, come on. If you don't," she warned, "I'll walk right up to the saloon with you."

He looked down at her, sudden panic within him. Although she was not his own daughter, he had always felt that she was. "No," he said sharply. "You mustn't."

"Then come with me," she insisted, grabbing his arm.

Still no sign of the Kid. Well, it would do no harm to wait, and he could at least get Ruth out of harm's way. He turned aside and went into the store with her. She had a new bridle she wanted him to see, and she wanted to know if he thought the bit was right for her mare. Deliberately she stalled. Once he looked up, thinking he heard riders. Then he replied to her questions. Finally he got away.

He stepped out into the sunlight, smelling dust in the air. Then he walked slowly across and up the street. As he reached the center of the street, the Mohave Kid came out of the Trail Driver and stepped off the walk, facing him.

Thirty yards separated them. Ab Kale waited, his keen blue eyes steady and cold. He must make this definite, and, if the Kid made the slightest move toward a gun, he must kill him. The sun was very warm.

"Kid," he said, "your business in town is finished. We don't want you here. Because of the family connection, I let you know that you weren't welcome. I wanted to avoid a showdown. Now I see you won't accept that, so I'm giving you exactly one hour to leave town. If you are here after that hour, or if you ever come again, I'll kill you."

The Mohave Kid started to speak, and then he stopped, frozen by a sudden movement.

From behind stores, from doorways, from alleys, stepped a dozen men. All held shotguns or rifles, all directed at the Kid. He stared at them in shocked disbelief. Johnny Holdstock—Alec and Dave Holdstock—Jim Gray, their cousin—Webb Dixon, a brother-in-law—and Myron Holdstock, the old bull of the herd.

Ab Kale was petrified. Then he remembered Riley on that racing horse and that today was old Myron's fortieth wedding anniversary, with half the family at the party.

The Mohave Kid stared at them, his face turning gray and then dark with sullen fury.

"You do like the marshal says, Kid." Old Myron Holdstock's voice rang in the streets. "We've protected ye because you're one of our'n. But you don't start trouble with another of our'n. You git on your hoss an' git. Don't you ever show hide nor hair around here again."

The Mohave Kid's face was a mask of fury. He turned deliberately and walked to his horse. No man could face all those guns, and, being of Holdstock blood, he knew what would come if he tried to face them down. They would kill him.

He swung into the saddle, cast one black, bleak look at Ab Kale, and then rode out of town.

Slowly Kale turned to Holdstock, who had been standing in the door of his shop. "You needn't have done that," he said, "but I'm glad you did. . . .

Three days went by slowly, and then the rains broke. It began to pour shortly before daybreak and continued to pour. The washes were running bank full by noon, and the street was deserted. Kale left his office early and stepped outside, buttoning his slicker. The street was running with water, and a stream of rain was cutting a ditch under the corner of the office. Getting a shovel from the stable, he began to divert the water.

Up the street at the gun shop, Riley McClean got to his feet and took off the leather apron in which he worked. He was turning toward the door when it darkened suddenly and he looked up to see the bleak, rain-wet face of the Mohave Kid.

The Kid stared at him. "I've come for my gun," he said.

"That'll be two dollars," Riley said coolly.

"That's a lot, ain't it?"

"It's my price to you."

The Kid's flat eyes stared at him, and his shoulder seemed to hunch. Then from the tail of his eye he caught the movement of the marshal as he started to work with the shovel. Quickly he forked out $2 and slapped it on the counter. Then he fed five shells into the gun and stepped to the door. He took two quick steps and vanished.

Surprised, Riley started around the counter after him. But as he reached the end of the counter, he heard the Kid yell: "Ab!"

Kale, his slicker buttoned over his gun, looked around at the call. Frozen with surprise, he saw the Mohave Kid standing there, gun in hand. The Kid's flat face was grinning with grim triumph. And then the Kid's gun roared, and Ab Kale took a step backward and fell, facedown in the mud.

The Mohave Kid laughed suddenly, sardonically. He dropped his gun into his holster and started for the horse tied across the street.

He had taken but one step when Riley McClean spoke: "All right, Kid, here it is!"

The Mohave Kid whirled sharply to see the gunsmith standing in the doorway. The rain whipping against him, Riley McClean looked at the Kid. "Ab was my friend," he said. "I'm going to marry Ruth."

The Kid reached then, and in one awful, endless moment of realization he knew what Ab Kale had known for these several months, that Riley McClean was a man born to the gun. Even as the Kid's hand slapped leather, he saw Riley's weapon clearing and coming level. The gun steadied, and for that endless instant the Kid stared into the black muzzle. Then his own iron was clear and swinging up, and Riley's gun was stabbing flame.

The bullets, three of them fired rapidly, smashed the Mohave Kid in and around the heart. He took a step back, his own gun roaring and the bullet plowing mud, and then he went to his knees as Riley walked toward him, his gun poised for another shot. As the Kid died, his brain flared with realization, with knowledge of death, and he fell forward, sprawling on his face in the street. A rivulet, diverted by his body, curved around him, ran briefly red, and then trailed on.

People were gathering, but Riley McClean walked to Ab Kale. As he reached him, the older man stirred slightly.

Dropping to his knees, Riley turned him over. The marshal's eyes flickered open. There was a cut from the hairline on the side of his head in front that ran all along his scalp. The shattered end of the shovel handle told the story. Striking the shovel handle, which had been in front of his heart at the moment of impact, the bullet had glanced upward, knocking him out and ripping a furrow in his scalp.

Ab Kale got slowly to his feet and stared up the muddy street where the crowd clustered about the Mohave Kid.

"You killed him?"

"Had to. I thought he'd killed you."

Ab nodded. "You've got a fast hand. I've known it for months. I hope you'll never have to kill another man."

"I won't," Riley said quietly. "I'm not even going to carry a gun after this."

Ab Kale glanced back up the street. "So he's dead at last. I've carried that burden a long time." He looked up, his face still white with shock. "They'll bury him. Let's go home, son. The women will be worried."

And the two men walked down the street side by side, Ab Kale and his son. . . .

West Is Where
the Heart Is

Jim London lay facedown in the dry prairie grass, his body pressed tightly against the ground. Heat, starvation, and exhaustion had taken a toll of his lean, powerful body, and, although light-headed from their accumulative effects, he still grasped the fact that to survive he must not be seen.

Hot sun blazed upon his back, and in his nostrils was the stale, sour smell of clothes and body long unwashed. Behind him lay days of dodging Comanche war parties and sleeping on the bare ground behind rocks or under bushes. He was without weapons or food, and it had been nine hours since he had tasted water, and that was only dew he had licked from leaves.

The screams of the dying rang in his ears, amid the sounds of occasional shots and the shouts and war cries of the Indians. From a hill almost five miles away he had spotted the white canvas tops of the Conestoga wagons and had taken a course that would intercept them. And then, in the last few minutes before he could reach their help, the Comanches had hit the wagon train.

From the way the attack went, a number of the

Indians must have been bedded down in the tall grass, keeping out of sight, and then, when the train was passing, they sprang for the drivers of the teams. The strategy was perfect, for there was then no chance of the wagon train making its circle. The lead wagons did swing, but two other teamsters were dead and another was fighting for his life, and their wagons could not be turned. The two lead wagons found themselves isolated from the last four and were hit hard by at least twenty Indians. The wagon whose driver was fighting turned over in the tall grass at the edge of a ditch, and the driver was killed.

Within twenty minutes after the beginning of the attack, the fighting was over and the wagons looted, and the Indians were riding away, leaving behind them only dead and butchered oxen, the scalped and mutilated bodies of the drivers, and the women who were killed or who had killed themselves.

Yet Jim London did not move. This was not his first crossing of the plains or his first encounter with Indians. He had fought Comanches before, as well as Kiowas, Apaches, Sioux, and Cheyennes. Born on the Oregon Trail, he had later been a teamster on the Santa Fe. He knew better than to move now. He knew that an Indian or two might come back to look for more loot.

The smoke of the burning wagons bit at his nostrils, yet he waited. An hour had passed before he let himself move, and then it was only to inch to the top of the hill, where from behind a tuft of bunch grass he surveyed the scene before him.

No living thing stirred near the wagons. Slow tendrils of smoke lifted from blackened timbers and wheel spokes. Bodies lay scattered about, grotesque in attitudes of tortured death. For a long time he studied the scene below, and the surrounding hills. And then he crawled over the skyline and slithered downhill through the grass, making no more visible disturbance than a snake or a coyote.

This was not the first such wagon train he had come upon, and he knew there was every chance that he would find food among the ruins as well as water, perhaps even overlooked weapons. Indians looted hastily and took the more obvious things, usually scattering food and wasting what they could not easily carry away.

Home was still more than two hundred miles away, and the wife he had not seen in four years would be waiting for him. In his heart, he knew she would be waiting. During the war the others had scoffed at him.

"Why, Jim, you say yourself she don't even know where you're at. She probably figures you're dead. No woman can be expected to wait that long. Not for a man she never hears of and when she's in a good country for men and a bad one for women."

"She'll wait. I know Jane."

"No man knows a woman that well. No man could. You say yourself you come East with a wagon train in 'sixty-one. Now it's 'sixty-four. You been in the war, you been wounded, you ain't been home, nor heard from her, nor she from you.

Worst of all, she was left on a piece of ground with only a cabin built, no ground broke, no close up neighbors. I'll tell you, Jim, you're crazy. Come, go to Mexico with us."

"No," he had said stubbornly. "I'll go home. I'll go back to Jane. I came East after some fixings for her, after some stock for the ranch, and I'll go home with what I set out after."

"You got any young 'uns?" The big sergeant had been skeptical.

"Nope. I sure ain't, but I wish I did. Only," he had added, "maybe I have. Jane, she was expecting, but had a time to go when I left. I only figured to be gone four months."

"And you been gone four years?" The sergeant had shook his head. "Forget her, Jim, and come with us. Nobody would deny she was a good woman. From what you tell of her, she sure was, but she's been alone and no doubt figures you're dead. She'll be married again, maybe with a family."

Jim London had shaken his head. "I never took up with no other woman, and Jane wouldn't take up with any other man. I'm going home."

He had made a good start. He had saved nearly every dime of pay, and he did some shrewd buying and trading when the war was over. He started West with a small but good train, and he had two wagons with six head of mules to the wagon, knowing the mules would sell better in New Mexico than would oxen. He had six cows and a yearling bull, some pigs, chickens, and utensils. He was a proud man when he looked over his outfit, and he hired two boys with the train to help him with the extra wagon and the stock.

Comanches hit them before they were well started. They killed two men and one woman, and stampeded some stock. The wagon train continued, and at the forks of Little Creek they struck again, in force this time, and only Jim London came out of it alive. All his outfit was gone, and he escaped without weapons, food, or water.

He lay flat in the grass at the edge of the burned spot. Again he studied the hills, and then he eased forward and got to his feet. The nearest wagon was upright, and smoke was still rising from it. The wheels were partly burned, the box badly charred, and the interior smoking. It was still too hot to touch.

He crouched near the front wheel and studied the situation, avoiding the bodies. No weapons were in sight, but he had scarcely expected any. There had been nine wagons. The lead wagons were thirty or forty yards off, and the three wagons whose drivers had been attacked were bunched in the middle with one overturned. The last four, near one of which he was crouched, had burned further than the others.

Suddenly he saw a dead horse lying at one side with a canteen tied to the saddle. He crossed to it at once, and, tearing the canteen loose, he rinsed his mouth with water. Gripping himself tight against drinking, he rinsed his mouth again and moistened his cracked lips. Only then did he let a mere swallow trickle down his parched throat.

Resolutely he put the canteen down in the shade

and went through the saddle pockets. It was a treasure trove. He found a good-size chunk of almost iron-hard brown sugar, a half dozen biscuits, a chunk of jerky wrapped in paper, and a new plug of chewing tobacco. Putting these things with the canteen, he unfastened the slicker from behind the saddle and added that to the pile.

Wagon by wagon he searched, always alert to the surrounding country and at times leaving the wagons to observe the plain from a hilltop. It was quite dark before he was finished. Then he took his first good drink, for he had allowed himself only nips during the remainder of the day. He took his drink, and then ate a biscuit, and chewed a piece of the jerky. With his hunting knife he shaved a little of the plug tobacco and made a cigarette by rolling it in paper, the way the Mexicans did.

Every instinct warned him to be away from the place by daylight, and, as much as he disliked leaving the bodies as they were, he knew it would be folly to bury them. If the Indians passed that way again, they would find them buried and would immediately be on his trail.

Crawling along the edge of the taller grass near the depression where the wagon had tipped over, he stopped suddenly. Here in the ground near the edge of the grass was a boot print!

His fingers found it, and then felt carefully. It had been made by a running man, either large or heavily laden. Feeling his way along the tracks, London stopped again, for this time his hand had come in contact with a boot. He shook it, but there was no move or response. Crawling nearer he touched the man's hand. It was cold as marble in the damp night air.

Moving his hand again, he struck canvas. Feeling along it he found it was a long canvas sack. Evidently the dead man had grabbed this sack from the wagon and dashed for the shelter of the ditch or hollow. Apparently he had been struck by a bullet and killed, but, feeling again of the body, London's hand came in contact with a belt gun. So the Comanches had not found him! Stripping the belt and gun from the dead man, London swung it around his own hips, and then checked the gun. It was fully loaded, and so were the cartridge loops in the belt.

Something stirred in the grass, and instantly he froze, sliding out his hunting knife. He waited for several minutes, and then he heard it again. Something alive lay here in the grass with him!

A Comanche? No Indian likes to fight at night, and he had seen no Indians anywhere near when darkness fell. No, if anything lived near him now, it must be something, man or animal, from the wagon train. For a long time he lay still, thinking it over, and then he took a chance. Yet from his experience the chance was not a long one.

"If there is someone there, speak up."

There was no sound, and he waited, listening. Five minutes passed—ten—twenty. Carefully, then, he slid through the grass, changing his position, and then froze in place. Something was moving, quite near!

His hand shot out, and he was shocked to find himself grasping a small hand with a ruffle of cloth at the wrist! The child struggled violently, and he whispered hoarsely: "Be still. I'm a friend. If you run, the Indians might come." Instantly the struggling stopped. "There," he breathed. "That's better." He searched his mind for something reassuring to say, and finally said: "Damp here, isn't it? Don't you have a coat?"

There was a momentary silence, and then a small voice said: "It was in the wagon."

"We'll look for it pretty soon," London said. "My name's Jim. What's yours?"

"Betty Jane Jones. I'm five years old and my papa's name is Daniel Jones and he is forty-six. Are you forty-six?"

London grinned. "No, I'm just twenty-nine, Betty Jane." He hesitated a minute, and then said: "Betty Jane, you strike me as a mighty brave little girl. There when I first heard you, you made no more noise than a rabbit. Now do you think you can keep that up?"

"Yes." It was a very small voice but it sounded sure.

"Good. Now listen, Betty Jane." Quietly he told her where he had come from and where he was going. He did not mention her parents, and she did not ask about them. From that he decided she knew only too well what had happened to them and the others from the wagon train.

"There's a canvas sack here, and I've got to look into it. Maybe there's something we can use. We're going to need food, Betty Jane, and a rifle. Later, we're going to have to find horses and money."

The sound of his voice, low though it was, seemed to give her confidence. She crawled nearer to him, and, when she felt the sack, she said: "That's Daddy's bag. He keeps his carbine in it and his best clothes."

"Carbine?" London fumbled open the sack.

"Is a carbine like a rifle?"

He told her it was, and then found the gun. It was carefully wrapped, and by the feel of it London could tell the weapon was new or almost new. There was ammunition, another pistol, and a small canvas sack that chinked softly with gold coins. He stuffed this in his pocket. A careful check of the remaining wagons netted him nothing more, but he was not disturbed. The guns he had were good ones, and he had a little food and the canteen. Gravely he took Betty Jane's hand and they started.

They walked for an hour before her steps began to drag, and then he picked her up and carried her. By the time the sky had grown gray, he figured they had come six or seven miles from the burned wagons. He found some solid ground among some reeds on the edge of a slough, and they settled down there for the day.

After making coffee with a handful found in one of the only partly burned wagons, London gave Betty Jane some of the jerky and a biscuit. Then for the first time he examined his carbine. His eyes brightened as he sized it up. It was a Ball & Lamson Repeating Carbine, a gun just on the market and of which this must have been one of the first sold. It was a seven-shot weapon carrying a .56-50 cartridge. It was almost thirty-eight inches in length and weighed a bit over seven pounds.

The pistols were also new, both Prescott Navy six-shooters, caliber .38 with rosewood grips. Betty Jane looked at them and tears welled into her eyes. He took her hand quickly.

"Don't cry, honey. Your dad would want me to use the guns to take care of his girl. You've been mighty brave. Now keep it up."

She looked up at him with woebegone eyes, but the tears stopped, and after a while she fell asleep.

There was little shade, and, as the reeds were not tall, he did not dare stand up. They kept close to the edge of the reeds and lay perfectly still. Once he heard a horse walking not far away and heard low, guttural voices and a hacking cough. He caught only a fleeting glimpse of one rider and hoped the Indians would not find their tracks.

When night came, they started on once more. He took his direction by the stars and he walked steadily, carrying Betty Jane most of the distance. Sometimes when she walked beside him, she talked. She rambled on endlessly about her home, her dolls, and her parents. Then on the third day she mentioned Hurlburt.

"He was a bad man. My papa told Mama he was a bad man. Papa said he was after Mister Ballard's money."

"Who was Hurlburt?" London asked, more to keep the child occupied than because he wanted to know.

"He tried to steal Daddy's new carbine, and Mister Ballard said he was a thief. He told him so."

Hurlburt. The child might be mispronouncing the name, but it sounded like that. There had been a man in Independence by that name. He had not been liked—a big, bearded man, very quarrelsome.

"Did he have a beard, Betty Jane? A big, black beard?"

She nodded eagerly. "At first, he did. But he didn't have it when he came back with the Indians."

"What?" He turned so sharply toward her that her eyes widened. He put his hand on her shoulder. "Did you say this Hurlburt came back with the Indians?"

Seriously she nodded. "I saw him. He was in back of them, but I saw him. He was the one who shot his gun at Mister Ballard."

"You say he came back?" London asked. "You mean he went away from the wagons before the attack?"

She looked at him. "Oh, yes! He went away when we stopped by the big pool. Mister Ballard and Daddy caught him taking things again. They put ropes on him, on his hands and his feet. But when morning came, I went to see, and he was gone away. Daddy said he had left the wagons, and he hoped nothing would happen to him."

Hurlburt. He had gone away and then had come back with the Indians. A renegade, then. What had they said of him in Independence? He had been over the trail several times. Maybe he was working with the Indians.

Betty Jane went to sleep on the grass he had pulled for her to lie on, and Jim London made a careful reconnaissance of the area, and then returned and lay down himself. After a long time he dozed, dreaming of Jane. He awakened feeling discouraged, with the last of their food gone. He had not tried the rifle, although twice they had seen antelope. There was too much chance of being heard by Indians.

Betty Jane was noticeably thinner, and her face looked wan as she slept. Suddenly he heard a sound and looked up, almost too late. Not a dozen feet away a Comanche looked over the reeds and aimed a rifle at him! Hurling himself to one side, he jerked out one of the Navy pistols. The Comanche's rifle bellowed, and then Jim fired. The Indian threw up his rifle and fell over backward and lay still.

Carefully London looked around. The rim of the hills was unbroken, and there was no other Indian in sight. The Indian's spotted pony cropped grass not far away. Gun in hand, London walked to the Indian. The bullet from the pistol had struck him under the chin and, tearing out the back, had broken the man's neck. A scarcely dry scalp was affixed to his rawhide belt, and the rifle he carried was new.

He walked toward the horse. The animal shied back. "Take it easy, boy," London said softly. "You're all right." Surprisingly the horse perked up both ears and stared at him.

"Understand English, do you?" he said softly. "Well, maybe you're a white man's horse. We'll see."

He caught the reins and held out a hand to the horse. It hesitated, and then snuffed of his fingers. He moved up the reins to it and touched a palm to the animal's back. The bridle was a white man's, too. There was no saddle, however, only a blanket.

Betty Jane was crying softly when he reached her, obviously frightened by the guns. He picked her up, and then the rifle, and started back toward the horse. "Don't cry, honey. We've got a horse now."

She slept in his arms that night, and he did not stop riding. He rode all through the night until the little horse began to stumble, and then he dismounted and led the horse while Betty Jane rode. Just before daylight they rested.

Two days later, tired, unshaven, and bedraggled, Jim London rode down the dusty street of Cimarron toward the Maxwell House. It was bright in the afternoon sunlight, and the sun glistened on the flanks and shoulders of the saddled horses at the hitch rail. Drawing up before the house, London slid from the saddle. Maxwell was standing on the wide porch, staring down at him, and beside him was Tom Boggs, who London remembered from Missouri as the grandson of Daniel Boone.

"You look plumb tuckered, stranger, and that looks like an Injun rig on the horse. Or part of it."

"It is. The Indian's dead." He looked at Maxwell. "Is there a woman around here? This kid's nigh dead for rest and comfort."

"Sure!" Maxwell exclaimed heartily. "Lots of women around. My wife's inside." He took the sleeping child and called to his wife. As he did so, the child's eyes opened and stared, and then the corners of her mouth drew down and she screamed. All three men turned to where she looked. Hurlburt was standing there, gaping at the child as if the earth had opened before him.

"What is it?" Maxwell looked perplexed. "What's the matter?"

"That's the man who killed Mister Ballard! I saw him!"

Hurlburt's face paled. "*Aw*, the kid's mistook me for somebody else," he scoffed. "I never seen her before." He turned to Jim London. "Where'd you find that youngster?" he demanded. "Who are you?"

Jim London did not immediately reply. He was facing Hurlburt and suddenly all his anger and irritation at the trail, the Indians, the awful butchery around the wagons returned to him and boiled down to this man. A child without parents because of this man.

"I picked that child up on the ground near a burned-out, Indian-raided wagon train," he said. "The same train you left Missouri with."

Hurlburt's face darkened with angry blood.

"You lie," he declared viciously. "You lie!"

Jim did not draw. He stared at Hurlburt, his eyes unwavering. "How'd you get here, then? You were in Independence when I left there. No wagons passed us. You had to be with that Ballard train."

"I ain't been in Independence for two years,"

Hurlburt blustered. "You're crazy and so's that blasted kid."

"Seems kind of funny," Maxwell suggested, his eyes cold. "You sold two rifles after you got here, and you had gold money. There's a train due in, the boys tell me. Maybe we better hold you until we ask them if you were in Independence."

"Like hell!" Hurlburt said furiously. "I ain't no renegade, and nobody holds me in no jail!"

Jim London took an easy step forward. "These guns I'm wearing, Hurlburt, belonged to Jones. I reckon he'd be glad to see this done. You led those Indians against those wagons. They found out you were a thief and faced you with it. I got it from Betty Jane, and the kid wouldn't lie about a thing like that. She told me all about it before we got here. So you don't get to go to jail. You don't get to wait. You get a chance to reach for a gun, and that's all."

Hurlburt's face was ugly. Desperately he glanced right and left. A crowd had gathered, but nobody spoke for him. He was up against it and he knew it. Suddenly he grabbed for his guns. Jim London's Prescott Navies leaped from their holsters, and the right one barked, a hard sharp report. Hurlburt backed up two steps, and then fell facedown, a blue hole over his eye.

"Good work," Boggs said grimly. "I've had my doubts about that *hombre*. He never does nothing, but he always has money."

"Staying around?" Maxwell asked, looking at London.

"No," Jim said quietly. "My wife's waiting for me. I ain't seen her since 'sixty-one."

"Since 'sixty-one?" Boggs was incredulous. "You heard from her?"

"She didn't know where I was. Anyway, she never learned to write none." He flushed slightly. "I can't, neither. Only my name."

Lucian Maxwell looked away, clearing his throat. Then he said very carefully: "Better not rush any, son. That's a long time. It'll soon be five years."

"She'll be waiting." He looked at them, one to the other. "It was the war. They took me in the Army, and I fought all through."

"What about the kid?" Boggs asked.

"Come morning she'll be ready, I reckon. I'll take her with me. She'll need a home, and I sort of owe her something for this here rifle and the guns. Also"—he looked at them calmly—"I got nine hundred dollars in gold and bills here in my pocket. It's hers. I found it in her daddy's duffel." He cleared his throat. "I reckon that'll buy her a piece of any place we got and give her a home with us for life. We wanted a little girl, and while my wife . . . she was expecting . . . I don't know if anything come of it."

Both men were silent, and finally Maxwell said: "See here, London, your wife may be dead. She may have married again. Anyway, she couldn't have stayed on that ranch alone. Man, you'd better leave the child here with us. Take the money. You earned it, packing her here, but let her stay until you find out."

London shook his head patiently. "You don't understand," he said, "that's my Jane who's waiting. She told me she'd wait for me, and she don't say things light. Not her."

"Where is she?" Maxwell asked curiously.

"We got us a place up on North Fork. Good grass, water, and timber. The wife likes trees. I built us a cabin there, and a lean-to. We aimed to put about forty acres to wheat and maybe set us up a mill." He looked up at them, smiling a little. "Pa was a miller, and he always said to me that folks need bread wherever they are. 'Make a good loaf,' he said, 'and you'll always have a good living.' He had him a mill up Oregon way."

"North Fork?" Boggs and Maxwell exchanged glances. "Man, that country was run over by Injuns two years ago. Some folks went back up there, but one o' them is Bill Ketchum. He's got a bunch running with him no bettern'n he is. Hoss thieves, folks reckon. Most anything to get the 'coon."

When he rounded the bend below the creek and saw the old bridge ahead of him, his mouth got dry and his heart began to pound. He walked his horse, with the child sitting before him and the carbine in its scabbard. At the creek he drew up for just a moment, looking down at the bridge. He had built it with his own hands. Then his eyes saw the hand rail on the right. It was cut from a young poplar. He had used cedar. Somebody had worked on that bridge recently.

The cabin he had built topped a low rise in a clearing backed by a rocky overhang. He rode through the pines, trying to quiet himself. It might be like they said. Maybe she had sold out and gone away, or just gone. Maybe she had married somebody else, or maybe the Indians. . . .

The voice he heard was coarse and amused. "Come off it!" the voice said. "From here on you're my woman. I ain't takin' no more of this guff!"

Jim London did not stop his horse when it entered the clearing. He let it walk right along, but he lifted the child from in front of him and said: "Betty Jane, that lady over yonder is your new ma. You run to her now, an' tell her your name is Jane. Hear me?"

He lowered the child to the ground and she scampered at once toward the slender woman with the wide gray eyes who stood on the step staring at the rider.

Bill Ketchum turned abruptly to see what her expression meant. The lean, raw-boned man on the horse had a narrow sun-browned face and a battered hat pulled low. The rider shoved it back now and rested his right hand on his thigh. Ketchum stared at him. Something in that steel-trap jaw and those hard eyes sent a chill through him.

"I take it," London said gravely, "that you are Bill Ketchum. I heard what you said just now. I also heard down the line that you were a horse thief, maybe worse. You get off this place now, and don't ever come back. You do and I'll shoot you on sight. Now get!"

"You talk mighty big." Ketchum stared at him, anger rising within him. Should he try this fellow? Who did he think he was, anyway?

"I'm big as I talk," London said flatly. "I done

killed a man yesterday down to Maxwell's. *Hombre* name of Hurlburt. That's all I figure to kill this week unless you want to make it two. Start moving now."

Ketchum hesitated, then viciously reined his horse around and started down the trail. As he neared the edge of the woods, rage suddenly possessed him. He grabbed for his rifle and instantly a shot rang out and a heavy slug gouged the butt of his rifle and glanced off.

Beyond him the words were plain. "I put that one right where I wanted it. This here's a seven-shot repeater, so if you want one through your heart, just try it again."

London waited until the man had disappeared in the trees, and a minute more. Only then did he turn to his wife. She was down on the step with her arm around Betty Jane, who was sobbing happily against her breast.

"Jim," she whispered. "Oh, Jim."

He got down heavily. He started toward her, and then stopped. Around the corner came a boy of four or five, a husky youngster with a stick in his hand and his eyes blazing. When he saw Jim, he stopped abruptly. This stranger looked just like the old picture on his mother's table. Only he had on a coat in the picture, a store-bought coat.

"Jim." Jane was on her feet now, color coming back into her face. "This is Little Jim. This is your son."

Jim London swallowed and his throat suddenly filled. He looked at his wife and started toward her. He felt awkward, clumsy. He took her by the elbows. "Been a long time, honey," he said hoarsely, "a mighty long time."

She drew back a little nervously. "Let's . . . I've coffee on. We'll. . . ." She turned and hurried toward the door, and he followed.

It would take some time. A little time for both of them to get over feeling strange, and maybe more time for her. She was a woman, and women needed time to get used to things.

He turned his head and almost automatically his eyes went to that south forty. The field was green with a young crop. Wheat! He smiled.

She had filled his cup; he dropped into a seat, and she sat down opposite him. Little Jim looked awkwardly at Betty Jane, and she stared at him with round, curious eyes.

"There's a big frog down by the bridge," Little Jim said suddenly. "I bet I can make him hop."

They ran outside into the sunlight, and across the table Jim London took his wife's hand. It was good to be home. Mighty good.

Home in the Valley

Steve Mehan placed the folded newspaper beside his plate and watched the waiter pour his coffee. He was filled with that warm, expansive glow that comes only from a job well done, and he felt he had just cause to feel it.

Jake Hitson, the money-lending rancher from down at the end of Paiute Valley, had sneered when he heard of the attempt, and the ranchers had shaken their heads doubtfully when Steve first told them of his plan. They had agreed only because there was no alternative. He had proposed to drive a herd of cattle from the Nevada range to California in the dead of winter!

To the north the passes were blocked with snow, and to the south lay miles of trackless and almost waterless desert. Yet they had been obligated to repay the money Hitson had loaned them by the first day of March or lose their ranches to him. It had been a pitifully small amount when all was considered, yet Hitson had held their notes, and he had intended to have their range.

Months before, returning to Nevada, Steve Mehan had scouted the route. The gold rush was in full swing, people were crowding into California, and there was a demand for beef. As a boy he had packed and freighted over most of the trails and knew them well, so finally the ranchers had given in.

The drive had been a success. With surprisingly few losses he had driven the herd into central California and had sold out, a few head here and a few there, and the prices had been good.

The five ranchers of Paiute Valley who had trusted their cattle to him were safe. $25,000 in $50 gold slugs had been placed on deposit in Dake & Company's bank here in Sacramento City.

With a smile, he lifted his coffee cup. Then, as a shadow darkened his table, he glanced up to see Jake Hitson.

The man dropped into a chair opposite him, and there was a triumphant light in his eyes that made Steve suddenly wary. Yet with the gold in the bank there was nothing to make him apprehensive.

"Well, you think you've done it, don't you?" Hitson's voice was malicious. "You think you've stopped me? You've played the hero in front of Betty Bruce, and the ranchers will welcome you back with open arms. You think when everything was lost you stepped in and saved the day?"

Mehan shrugged. "We've got the money to pay you, Jake. The five brands of the Paiute will go on. This year looks like a good one, and we can drive more cattle over the route I took this time, so they'll make it now. And that in spite of all the bad years and the rustling of your friends."

Hitson chuckled. He was a big man with straw-colored brows and a flat red face. From one small spread down there at the end of the Paiute he had expanded to take in a fair portion of the valley. The methods he had used would not bear examination, and strange cattle had continued to flow into the valley, enlarging his herds. Many of the brands were open to question. The hard years and losses due to cold or drought did not affect him, because he kept adding to his herds from other sources.

During the bad years he had loaned money, and his money had been the only help available. The fact that he was a man disliked for his arrogant manner and his crooked connections made the matter only the more serious.

Hitson grinned with malice. "Read your paper yet, Mehan? If you want to spoil your breakfast, turn to page three."

Steve Mehan's dark eyes held the small blue ones of Hitson, and he felt something sick and empty in his stomach. Only bad news for him could give Hitson the satisfaction he was so obviously feeling.

Yet, even as Steve opened the paper, a man bent over the table next to him.

"Heard the news?" he asked excitedly. "Latch and Evans banking house has failed. That means that Dake and Company are gone, too. They'll close the doors. There's already a line out there a hundred yards long and still growin'!"

Steve opened his paper slowly. The news was there for all to read. Latch & Evans had failed. The managing director had flown the coop, and only one interpretation could be put upon that. Dake & Company, always closely associated with Latch & Evans, would be caught in the collapse. February of 1855 would see the end of the five brands of Paiute Valley. It would be the end of everything he had planned, everything he wanted for Betty.

"See?" Hitson sneered, heaving himself to his feet. "Try and play hero now. I've got you and them highfalutin' friends of yours where I want 'em. I'll kick every cussed one of 'em into the trail on March first, and with pleasure. And that goes for you, Steve Mehan."

Steve scarcely heard him. He was remembering that awful drive. The hard winds, the bitter cold, the bawling cattle. And then the desert, the Indians, the struggle to get through with the herd intact—and all to end in this. Collapse and failure. Yes, and the lives of two men had been sacrificed, the two who had been killed on the way over the trail.

Mehan remembered Chuck Farthing's words. He had gone down with a Mojave Indian's bullet in his chest.

"Get 'em through, boy. Save the old man's ranch for him. That's all I ask."

It had been little enough for two lives. And now they were gone, for nothing.

The realization hit Steve Mehan like a blow and brought him to his feet fighting mad, his eyes blazing, his jaw set.

"I'll be eternally blasted if they have!" he exploded, although only he knew what he meant.

He started for the door, leaving his breakfast

unfinished behind him, his mind working like lightning. The whole California picture lay open for him now. The news of the failure would have reached the Dake & Company branches in Marysville and Grass Valley. And in Placerville. There was no hope there.

Portland? He stopped short, his eyes narrowed with thought. Didn't they have a branch in Portland? Of course! He remembered it well, now that he thought of it. The steamer from San Francisco would leave the next morning, and it would be carrying the news. But what if he could beat that steamer to Portland?

Going by steamer himself would be futile, for he would arrive at the same time the news did, and there would be no chance for him to get his money. Hurrying down the street, his eyes scanning the crowds for Pink Egan and Jerry Smith, cowpunchers who had made the drive with him, he searched out every possible chance, and all that remained was that seven hundred miles of trail between Sacramento and Portland, rough, and part of it harassed by warring Modocs.

He paused, glancing around. He was a tall young man with rusty brown hair and a narrow, rather scholarly face. To the casual observer he looked like a roughly dressed frontier doctor or lawyer. Actually he was a man bred to the saddle and the wild country.

Over the roofs of the buildings he could see the smoke of a steamboat. It was the stern-wheeler *Belle*, just about to leave for Knights Landing, forty-two miles upstream.

He started for the gangway, walking fast, and, just as he reached it, a hand caught his sleeve. He wheeled to see Pink and Jerry at his elbow.

"Hey!" Smith demanded. "Where you goin' so fast?"

"We run two blocks to catch up with you."

Quickly Steve explained. The riverboat tooted its whistle, and the crew started for the gangway to haul it aboard. "It's our only chance!" Steve Mehan exclaimed. "I've got to beat that steamboat from Frisco to Portland and draw my money before they get the news. Don't tell anybody where I've gone, and keep your eyes on Hitson."

He lunged for the gangway and raced aboard. It was foolish, it was wild, it was impossible, but it was their only chance. Grimly he recalled what he had told Betty Bruce when he left the valley. "I'll get them cattle over, honey, or I'll die trying."

"You come back, Steve," she had begged. "That's all I ask. We can always go somewhere and start over. We always have each other."

"I know, honey, but how about your father? How about Pete Farthing? They're too old to start over, and the ranches are all they have. They worked like slaves, fought Indians, gave a lot in sweat and blood for their ranches. I'll not see 'em turned out now. Whatever comes, I'll make it."

As the riverboat pushed away from the dock, he glanced back. Jake Hitson was staring after him, his brow furrowed. Jake had seen him, and that was bad.

Mehan put such thoughts behind him. The boat would not take long to get to Knights Landing, and he could depend upon Knight to help him. The man had migrated from New Mexico fifteen years before, but he had known Steve's father, and they had come over the Santa Fe Trail together. From a mud-and-wattle hut on an Indian mound at the landing, he had built a land grant he got from his Mexican wife into a fine estate, and the town had been named for him.

Would Jake Hitson guess what he was attempting? If so, what could he do? The man had money, and with money one can do many things. Hitson would not stop at killing. Steve had more than a hunch that Hitson had urged the Mojaves into the attack on the cattle drive that had resulted in the death of Chuck Farthing. He had more than a hunch that the landslide that had killed Dixie Rollins had been due to more than purely natural causes. But he could prove nothing.

His only chance was to reach Portland before the news did. He was not worried about their willingness to pay him the money. The banks made a charge of one half of one percent for all withdrawals over $1,000, and it would look like easy profit to the agent at the banking and express house.

Nor was it all unfamiliar country, for Steve had spent two years punching cows on ranches, prospecting and hunting through the northern valleys, almost as far as the Oregon line.

When the *Belle* shouldered her comfortable bulk against the landing at Knights, Mehan did not wait for the gangway. He grabbed the bulwark and vaulted ashore, landing on his hands and knees.

He found Knight standing on the steps of his home, looking down toward the river.

"A hoss, Steve?" Knight repeated. "Shorest thing you know. What's up?"

While Steve threw a saddle on a tall chestnut, he explained briefly.

"You'll never make it, boy," Knight protested. "It's a hard drive, and the Modocs are raidin' again." He chewed on his mustache as Steve swung into the saddle. "Boy," he said, "when you get to the head of Grand Island, see the judge. He's an old friend of mine, and he'll let you have a hoss. Good luck."

Steve wheeled the chestnut into the street and started north at a spanking trot. He kept the horse moving, and the long-legged chestnut had a liking for the trail. He moved out eagerly, seeming to catch some of the anxiety to get over the trail that filled his rider.

At the head of Grand Island, Steve swapped horses and started north again, holding grimly to the trail. There was going to be little time for rest and less time to eat. He would have to keep moving if he was going to make it. The trail over much of the country was bad, and the farther north he got toward the line, the worse it would be.

His friends on the ranches remembered him, and he repeatedly swapped horses and kept moving. The sun was setting in a rose of glory when he made his fourth change of mount near the Marysville Buttes. The purple haze of evening was gathering when he turned up the trail and lined out.

He had money with him, and he paid a bonus plus a blown horse when necessary. But the stockmen were natural allies, as were the freighters along the route, and they were always willing to help. After leaving Knights Landing he had told no one his true mission, his only explanation being that he was after a thief. In a certain sense, that was exactly true.

At 10:00 p.m., ten hours out of Sacramento, he galloped into the dark streets of Red Bluffs. No more than five minutes later, clutching a sandwich in his hand and with a fresh horse under him, he was off again.

Darkness closed around him, and the air was cool. He had no rifle with him, only the pistol he habitually wore and plenty of ammunition.

The air was so cold that he drew his coat around him, tucking it under and around his legs. He spoke softly to the horse, and its ears twitched. It was funny about a horse—how much they would give for gentleness. There was no animal that responded so readily to good treatment, and no other animal would run itself to death for a man—except, occasionally, a dog.

The hoofs of the horse beat a pounding rhythm upon the trail, and Steve leaned forward in the saddle, hunching himself against the damp chill and to cut wind resistance. His eyes were alert, although weariness began to dull his muscles and take the drive and snap from them.

Twenty miles out of Red Bluffs he glimpsed a fire shining through the trees. He slowed the horse, putting a hand on its damp neck. It was a campfire.

He could see the light reflecting from the front of a covered wagon, and he heard voices speaking. He rode nearer and saw the faces of the men come around toward him.

"Who's there?" A tall man stepped around the fire with a rifle in his hand.

"Mehan, a cattleman. I'm after a thief and need a fresh horse."

"Well, light and talk. You won't catch him on that hoss. Damn' fine animal," he added, "but you've shore put him over the road."

"He's got heart, that one!" Steve said, slapping the horse. "Plenty of it. Is that coffee I smell?"

The bearded man picked up the pot. "It shore is, pardner. Have some." He poured a cupful, handed it to Steve, and then strolled over to the horse. "Shucks, with a rubdown and a blanket he'll be all right. Tell you what I'll do. I've got a buckskin here that'll run till he drops. Give me twenty to boot and he's yours."

Mehan looked up. "Done, but you throw in a couple of sandwiches."

The bearded man chuckled. "Shore will." He glanced at the saddle as Steve began stripping it from the horse. "You've got no rifle?"

"No, only a pistol. I'll take my chances."

"Haven't got a rifle to spare, but I'll make you a deal on this." He handed Steve a four-barreled Braendlin repeating pistol. "Frankly, mister, I need money. Got my family down to Red Bluffs, and I don't want to come in broke."

"How much?"

"Another twenty?"

"Sure, if you've got ammunition for it."

"I've got a hundred rounds. And it goes with the gun." The man dug out the ammunition. "Joe, wrap up a couple of them sandwiches for the man. Got smokin'?"

"Sure thing." Steve swung into the saddle and pocketed the extra pistol. He put the ammunition in his saddlebags. "Good luck."

"Hope you catch him!" the man called.

Steve touched a spur lightly to the big buckskin and was gone in a clatter of hoofs. Behind him the fire twinkled lonesomely among the dark columns of the trees, and then as he went down beyond a rise, the light faded, and he was alone in the darkness, hitting the road at a fast trot.

Later, he saw the white radiance that preceded the moon, and something else—the white, gleaming peak of Mount Shasta, one of the most beautiful mountains in the world. Lifting its fourteen-thousand-foot peak above the surrounding country, it was like a throne for the Great Spirit of the Indians.

In darkness and moving fast, Steve Mehan rode down the trail into Shasta and then on to Whiskeytown.

A drunken miner lurched from the side of a building and flagged him down. "No use hurryin'," he said. "It ain't true!"

"What ain't true?" Steve stared at him. "What you talking about?"

"That Whiskey Creek. Shucks, it's got water in it just like any creek." He spat with disgust. "I come all the way down here from Yreka huntin' it."

"You came from Yreka?" Steve grabbed his shoulder. "How's the trail? Any Indians out?"

"Trail?" The miner spat. "There ain't no trail! A loose-minded mule walked through the brush a couple of times, that's all. Indians? Modocs? Man, the woods is full of 'em! Behind ever' bush! Scalp-huntin' bucks, young and old. If you're headin' that way, you won't get through. Your hair will be in a teepee 'fore two suns go down."

He staggered off into the darkness, trying a song that dribbled away and lost itself in the noise of the creek.

Mehan walked the horse down to the creek and let him drink.

"No whiskey, but we'll settle for water, won't we, Buck?"

The creek had its name, he remembered, from an ornery mule that lost the barrel from its pack. It broke in Whiskey Creek, which promptly drew a name upon itself.

Steve Mehan started the horse again, heading for the stage station at Tower House, some ten miles up the road. The buckskin was weary but game. Ahead of him and on his right still loomed the peak of Mount Shasta, seeming large in the occasional glimpses, even at the distance that still separated them.

He almost fell from his horse at Tower House, with dawn bright in the eastern sky beyond the ragged mountains. The stage tender blinked sleepy eyes at him and then at the horse.

"You've been givin' her blazes," he said. "In a mite of hurry?"

"After a thief," mumbled Steve.

The man scratched his grizzled chin. "He must be a goin' son-of-a-gun," he commented whimsically. "Want anything?"

"Breakfast and a fresh horse."

"Easy done. You ain't figurin' on ridin' north, are you? Better change your plans if you are, because the Modocs are out and they're in a killin' mood. No trail north of here, you know."

With a quick breakfast and what must have been a gallon of coffee under his belt, Steve Mehan swung into the saddle and started once more. The new horse was a gray and built for the trail. Steve was sodden with weariness, and at every moment his lids fluttered and started to close. But now, for a while at least, he dared not close them.

Across Clear Creek he rode into the uplands where no wagon road had ever been started. It was a rugged country, but one he remembered from the past, and he weaved around among the trees, following the thread of what might have been a trail. Into a labyrinth of cañons he rode, following the vague trail up the bottom of a gorge, now in the water, then out of it. Then he climbed a steep trail out of the gorge and headed out across the long rolling swell of a grass-covered mountainside.

The air was much colder now, and there was an occasional flurry of snow. At times he clung to the saddle horn, letting the horse find his own trail, just so that trail was north. He rode into the heavily forested sides of the Trinity Mountains, losing the trail once in the dimness under the tall firs and tamaracks, but keeping on his northern route. Eventually he again hit what must have been the trail.

His body ached, and he fought to keep his eyelids open. Once he dismounted and walked for several miles to keep himself awake and to give the horse a slight rest. Then he was back in the saddle and riding once more.

Behind him somewhere was Jake Hitson. Jake, he knew well, would not give up easily. If he guessed what Mehan was attempting, he would stop at nothing to prevent it. And yet there was no way of preventing it unless he came north with the boat and reached Portland before him. And that would do no good, for if the boat got to Portland before him, the news would be there, and nothing Hitson could do would be any worse than the arrival of that news.

Egan and Smith would have their eyes on Jake Hitson, but he might find some means of getting away. Certainly, Steve thought grimly, nothing on horseback was going to catch him now.

The wind grew still colder and howled mournfully under the dark, needled trees. He shivered and hunched his shoulders against the wind. Once, half alseep, he almost fell from the horse when the gray shied at a fleeing rabbit.

As yet there were no Indians. He peered ahead across the bleak and forbidding countryside, but it was empty. And then, not long later, he turned down a well-marked trail to Trinity Creek.

He swung down in front of a log bunkhouse. A miner was at the door.

"A hoss?" The miner chuckled. "Stranger, you're shore out of luck. There ain't a hoss hereabouts you could get for love or money."

Steve Mehan sagged against the building. "Mister," he mumbled, "I've just got to get a horse. I've got to."

"Sorry, son. There just ain't none. Nobody in town would give up his hoss right now, and they are mighty scarce at that. You'd better come in and have some coffee."

Steve stripped his saddle and bridle from his horse and walked into the house. He almost fell into a chair. Several miners playing cards looked up. "*Amigo,*" one of them said, "you'd better lay off that stuff."

Mehan's head came up heavily, and he peered at the speaker, a blond giant in a red-checked shirt.

"I haven't slept since I left Sacramento," he said. "Been in the saddle ever since."

"Sacramento?" The young man stared. "You must be crazy."

"He's chasin' a thief," said the miner Steve had first seen. He was bringing Steve a cup of coffee. "I'd want a man awful bad before I rode like that."

"I got to beat the steamer to Portland," Steve said. It was a lie in a way, but actually the truth. "If I don't, the fellow will get away with fifteen thousand dollars."

"Fifteen thou. . . ." The young man laid down his hand. "Brother," he said emphatically, "I'd ride, too."

Steve gulped the coffee and lurched to his feet.

"Got to find a horse," he said, and lunged outside.

It took him less than a half hour to prove to himself that it was an impossibility. Nobody would even consider selling a horse, and his own was in bad shape.

"Not a chance," they told him. "A man without a hoss in this country is through. No way in or out but on a hoss, and not an extry in town."

He walked back to the stable. One look at his own horse told him the animal was through. There was no chance to go farther with it. No matter what he might do, the poor creature could stagger no more than a few miles. It would be killing a good horse to no purpose. Disgusted and discouraged, numbed with weariness, he stood in the cold wind, rubbing his grizzled chin with a fumbling hand.

So this was the end. After all his effort, the drive over the mountains and desert, the long struggle to get back, and then this ride, and all for nothing. Back there in the Paiute the people he had left behind would be trusting him, keeping their faith. For no matter how much they were sure he would fail, their hopes must go with him. And now he had failed.

Wearily he staggered into the bunkhouse and dropped into his chair. He fumbled with the coffeepot and succeeded in pouring out a cupful. His legs and feet felt numb, and he had never realized a man could be so utterly, completely tired.

The young man in the checkered shirt looked around from his poker game.

"No luck, eh? You've come a long way to lose now."

Steve nodded bitterly. "That money belongs to my friends as well as me," he said. "That's the worst of it."

The blond young fellow laid down his hand and pulled in the chips. Then he picked up his pipe.

"My sorrel out there in the barn," he said, "is the best hoss on the Trinity. You take it and go, but man, you'd better get yourself some rest at Scott Valley. You'll die."

Mehan lunged to his feet, hope flooding the weariness from his body.

"How much?" he demanded, reaching for his pocket.

"Nothin'," the fellow said. "Only if you catch that thief, bring him back on my hoss, and I'll help you hang him. I promise you."

Steve hesitated. "What about the horse?"

"Bring him back when you come south," the fellow said, "and take care of him. He'll never let you down."

Steve Mehan rode out of Trinity Creek ten minutes later, and the sorrel took to the trail as if he knew all that was at stake, and pressed on eagerly for Scott Valley.

The cold was increasing as Steve Mehan rode farther north, and the wind was raw, spitting rain that seemed to be changing to snow. Head hunched behind the collar of his buffalo coat, Steve pushed on, talking low to the horse, whose ears twitched a response and who kept going, alternating between a fast walk and a swinging, space-eating trot.

Six hours out of Trinity Creek, Steve Mehan rode into Scott Valley.

The stage tender took one look at him and waved him to a bunk.

"Hit it, stranger," he said. "I'll care for your hoss!" Stumbling through a fog of exhaustion, Steve made the bunk and dropped into its softness. . . .

Steve Mehan opened his eyes suddenly, with the bright sunlight in his face. He glanced at his watch. It was noon.

Lunging to his feet, he pulled on his boots, which somebody had removed without awakening him, and reached for his coat. The heavy-set red-haired stage tender walked in and glanced at him.

"See you've got Joe Chalmers's hoss," he remarked, his thumbs in his belt. "How come?"

Steve looked up. "Chasing a thief. He let me have it."

"I know Chalmers. He wouldn't let Moses have this hoss to lead the Israelites out of Egypt. Not him. You've got some explainin' to do, stranger."

"I said he loaned me the horse," Steve said grimly. "I'm leaving him with you and I want to buy another to go on with. What have you got?"

Red was dubious. "Don't reckon I should sell you one. Looks mighty funny to me, you havin' Joe's hoss. Is Joe all right?"

"Well," Steve said wearily, "he was just collecting a pot levied by three treys when I talked to him, so I reckon he'll make out."

Red chuckled. "He's a poker-playin' man, that

one. Good man, too." He hesitated, and then shrugged. "All right. There's a blaze-faced black in the stable you can have for fifty dollars. Good horse, too. Better eat somethin'."

He put food on the table, and Steve ate too rapidly. He gulped some coffee, and then Red came out with a pint of whiskey.

"Stick this in your pocket, stranger. Might come in handy."

"Thanks." Mehan wiped his mouth and got to his feet. He felt better, and he walked to the door.

"You ain't got a rifle?" Red was frankly incredulous. "The Modocs will get you shore."

"Haven't seen hide nor hair of one yet," Steve said, smiling. "I'm beginning to think they've all gone East for the winter."

"Don't you think it." Red slipped a bridle on the black while Steve cinched up the saddle. "They are out, and things up Oregon way are bad off. They shore raised ructions up around Grave Creek, and all the country around the Klamath and the Rogue is harassed by 'em."

Somewhere out at sea the steamer would be plowing over the gray sea toward Astoria and the mouth of the Columbia. The trip from there up to the Willamette and Portland would not take long.

The black left town at a fast lope and held it. The horse was good, no question about it. Beyond Callahan's, Steve hit the old Applegate wagon trail and found the going somewhat better and pushed on. Just seventy hours out from Knights Landing he rode into Yreka.

After a quick meal, a drink, and a fresh horse, he mounted and headed out of town for the Oregon line. He rode through Humbug City and Hawkins-ville without a stop and followed a winding trail up the gorge of the Shasta.

Once, after climbing the long slope north of the Klamath, he glimpsed a party of Indians some distance away. They sighted him, for they turned their horses his way, but he rode on, holding his pace, and crossed Hungry Creek and left behind him the cairn that marked the boundary line of Oregon. He turned away from the trail then and headed into the back country, trying a cut-off for Bear Creek and the village of Jacksonville. Some-where, he lost the Indians.

He pushed on, and now the rain that had been falling intermittently turned to snow. It began to fall, thick and fast. He was riding out of the trees when on the white-flecked earth before him he saw a moccasin track with earth just tumbling into it from the edge.

Instantly he whipped his horse around and touched spurs to its flanks. The startled animal gave a great bound, and at the same instant a shot whipped by where he had been only a moment before. Then he was charging through brush, and the horse was dodging among the trees.

An Indian sprang from behind a rock and lifted a rifle. Steve drew and fired. The Indian threw his rifle away and rolled over on the ground, moaning.

Wild yells chorused behind him, and a shot cut the branches overhead. He fired again and then again.

Stowing the Smith & Wesson away, he whipped out the four-barreled Braendlin. Holding it ready, he charged out of the brush and headed across the open country. Behind him the Modocs were coming fast. His horse was quick and alert, and he swung it around a grove of trees and down into a gully. Racing along the bottom, he hit a small stream and began walking the horse carefully upstream. After making a half mile, he rode out again and took to the timber, reloading his other pistol.

Swapping horses at every chance, he pushed on. One hundred and forty-three hours out of Knights Landing, he rode into Portland. He had covered six hundred and fifty-five miles. He swung down and turned to the stable hand.

"That steamer in from Frisco?"

"Heard her whistle," said the man. "She's comin' up the river now."

But Steve had turned and was running fast.

The agent for the banking express company looked up and blinked when Steve Mehan lurched through the door.

"I'm buying cattle," Steve told him, "and need some money. Can you honor a certificate of deposit for me?"

"Let's see her."

Steve handed him the order and shifted restlessly. The man eyed the order for a long time, and then turned it over and studied the back. Finally, when Steve was almost beside himself with impatience, the agent looked up over his glasses at the bearded, hollow-eyed young man. "Reckon I can," he said. "Of course there's the deduction of one half of one percent for all amounts over a thousand dollars."

"Pay me," Steve said.

He leaned over the desk, and suddenly the deep-toned blast of the steamer's whistle rang through the room. The agent was putting stacks of gold on the table. He looked up.

"Well, what do you know? That's the steamer in. I reckon I better see about. . . ."

Whatever he was going to see about, Steve never discovered, for as the agent turned away, Steve reached out and collared him. "Pay me," he said sharply. "Pay me now."

The agent shrugged. "Well, all right. No need to get all fussed about it. Plenty of time."

He put out stacks of gold. Mentally Steve calculated the amount. When it was all there, he swept it into a sack—almost fifty pounds of gold. He slung the sack over his shoulder and turned toward the door.

A gun boomed, announcing the arrival of the steamer, as he stepped out into the street. Four men were racing up the street from the dock, and the man in the lead was Jake Hitson.

Hitson skidded to a halt when he saw Steve Mehan, and his face went dark with angry blood. The blue eyes frosted and he stood wide-legged, staring at the man who had beaten him to Portland.

"So!" His voice was a roar that turned the startled townspeople around. "Beat me here, did you? Got your money, have you?" He seemed unable to absorb the fact that he was beaten, that Mehan had made it through.

"Just so you won't kick anybody out of his home, Jake," Steve said quietly, "and I hope that don't hurt too much."

The small man in the black suit had gone around them and into the express company office. The other men were Pink Egan and a swarthy-faced man who was obviously a friend of Hitson's.

Hitson lowered his head. The fury seemed to go out of him as he stood there in the street with a soft rain falling over them.

"You won't get back there," he said in a dead, flat voice. "You done it, all right, but you'll never play the hero in Paiute, because I'm goin' to kill you."

"Like you killed Dixie and Chuck?" challenged Steve. "You did, you know. You started that landslide and the Mojaves."

Hitson made no reply. He merely stood there, a huge bull of a man, his frosty eyes bright and hard under the corn-silk eyebrows.

Suddenly his hand swept down.

When Steve had first sighted the man, he had lowered the sack of gold to the street. Now he swept his coat back and grabbed for his own gun. He was no gunfighter, and the glimpse of flashing speed from Hitson made something go sick within him, but his gun came up and he fired.

Hitson's gun was already flaming, and even as Steve pulled the trigger on his own gun, a bullet from Hitson's pistol knocked the Smith & Wesson spinning into the dust! Steve sprang back and heard the hard, dry laugh of triumph from Jake Hitson's throat.

"Now I'll kill you!" Hitson yelled.

The killer's eyes were cold as he lifted the pistol, but, even as it came level, Steve hurled himself to his knees and jerked out the four-barreled Braendlin.

Hitson swung the gun down on him, but, startled by Steve's movement, he swung too fast and shot too fast. The bullet ripped through the top of Mehan's shoulder, tugging hard at the heavy coat. Then Steve fired. He fired once, twice, three times, and then heaved himself erect and stepped to one side, holding his last shot ready, his eyes careful.

Hitson stood stockstill, his eyes puzzled. Blood was trickling from his throat, and there was a slowly spreading blot of blood on his white shirt. He tried to speak, but when he opened his mouth, blood frothed there, and he started to back up, frowning.

He stumbled and fell. Slowly he rolled over on his face in the street. Blood turned the gravel crimson, and rain darkened the coat on his back.

Only then did Steve Mehan look up. Pink Egan, his face cold, had a gun leveled at Hitson's companion. "You beat it," Pink said. "You get goin'!"

"Shore." The man backed away, staring at Hitson's body. "Shore, I'm gone. I don't want no trouble. I just come along, I. . . ."

The small man in black came out of the express office.

"Got here just in time," he said. "I'm the purser from the steamer. Got nearly a thousand out of that bank, the last anybody will get." He smiled at Mehan. "Won another thousand on your ride. I bet on you and got two to one." He chuckled. "Of course,

I knew we had soldiers to put ashore at two places coming north, and that helped. I'm a sporting man, myself." He clinked the gold in his sack and smiled, twitching his mustache with a white finger. "Up to a point," he added, smiling again. "Only up to a point."

Fork Your Own Broncs

Mac Marcy turned in the saddle and, resting his left hand on the cantle, glanced back up the arroyo. His lean, brown face was troubled. There were cattle here, all right, but too few.

At this time of day, late afternoon and very hot, there should have been a steady drift of cattle toward the water hole.

Ahead of him he heard a steer bawl and then another. Now what? Above the bawling of the cattle he heard another sound, a sound that turned his face gray with worry. It was the sound of hammers.

He needed nothing more to tell him what was happening. Jingle Bob Kenyon was fencing the water hole!

As he rounded the bend in the wash, the sound of hammers ceased for an instant, but only for an instant. Then they continued with their work.

Two strands of barbed wire had already been stretched tight and hard across the mouth of the wash. Several cowhands were stretching the third wire of what was obviously to be a four-wire fence.

Already Marcy's cattle were bunching near the fence, bawling for water.

As he rode nearer, two men dropped their hammers and lounged up to the fence. Marcy's eyes narrowed and his gaze shifted to the big man on the roan horse. Jingle Bob Kenyon was watching him with grim humor.

Marcy avoided the eyes of the two other men by the fence, Vin Ricker and John Soley, who could mean only one thing for him—trouble, bad trouble. Vin Ricker was a gun hand and a killer. John Soley was anything Vin told him to be.

"This is a rotten trick, Kenyon," Marcy declared angrily. "In this heat my herd will be wiped out."

Kenyon's eyes were unrelenting. "That's just tough," he stated flatly. "I warned you when you fust come in here to git out while the gittin' was good. You stayed on. You asked for it. Now you take it or git out."

Temper flaring within him like a burst of flame, Marcy glared. But deliberately he throttled his fury. He would have no chance here. Ricker and Soley were too much for him, let alone the other hands and Kenyon himself.

"If you don't like it," Ricker sneered, "why don't you stop us? I hear tell you're a plumb salty *hombre*."

"You'd like me to give you a chance to kill me, wouldn't you?" Marcy asked harshly. "Someday I'll get you without your guns, Ricker, and I'll tear down your meat house."

Ricker laughed. "I don't want to dirty my hands on you, or I'd come over an' make you eat those words. If you ever catch me without these guns, you'll wish to old Harry I still had 'em."

Marcy turned his eyes away from the gunman and looked at Kenyon.

"Kenyon, I didn't think this of you. Without water, my cows won't last three days, and you know it. You'll bust me flat."

Kenyon was unrelenting. "This is a man's country, Marcy," he said dryly. "You fork your own bronc's an' you git your own water. Don't come whinin' to me. You moved in on me, an', if you git along, it'll be on your own."

Kenyon turned his horse and rode away. For an instant Marcy stared after him, seething with rage. Then, abruptly, he wheeled his grayish black horse—a moros—and started back up the arroyo. Even as he turned, he became aware that only six lean steers faced the barbed wire.

He had ridden but a few yards beyond the bend when that thought struck him like a blow. Six head of all the hundreds he had herded in here. By rights they should all be at the water hole or heading that way. Puzzled, he started back up the trail.

By rights, there should be a big herd here. Where could the cattle be? As he rode back toward his claim shack, he stared about him. No cattle were in sight. His range was stripped.

Rustlers? He scowled. But there had been no rustling activity of which he had heard. Ricker and Soley were certainly the type to rustle cattle, but Marcy knew Kenyon had been keeping them busy on the home range.

He rode back toward the shack, his heart heavy.

He had saved for seven years, riding cattle trails to Dodge, Abilene, and Ellsworth to get the money to buy his herd. It was his big chance to have a spread of his own, a chance for some independence and a home.

A home. He stared bitterly at the looming rimrock behind his outfit. A home meant a wife, and there was only one girl in the world for him. There would never be another who could make him feel as Sally Kenyon did. But she would have to be old Jingle Bob's daughter.

Not that she had ever noticed him. But in those first months before the fight with Jingle Bob became dog-eat-dog, Marcy had seen her around, watched her, been in love with her from a distance. He had always hoped that when his place had proved up and he was settled, he might know her better. He might even ask her to marry him.

It had been a foolish dream. Yet day by day it became even more absurd. He was not only in a fight with her father, but he was closer than ever to being broke.

Grimly, his mind fraught with worry, he cooked his meager supper, crouching before the fireplace. Again and again the thought kept recurring—where were his cattle? If they had been stolen, they would have to be taken down past the water hole and across Jingle Bob's range. There was no other route from Marcy's corner of range against the rim. For a horseman, yes. But not for cattle.

The sound of a walking horse startled him. He straightened, and then stepped away from the fire and put the bacon upon the plate, listening to the horse as it drew nearer. Then he put down his food, and, loosening his gun, he stepped to the door.

The sun had set long since, but it was not yet dark. He watched a gray horse coming down from the trees leading up to the rim. Suddenly he gulped in surprise.

It was Sally Kenyon! He stepped outside and walked into the open. The girl saw him and waved a casual hand, and then reined in.

"Have you a drink of water?" she asked, smiling. "It's hot, riding."

"Sure," he said, trying to smile. "Coffee, if you want. I was just fixing to eat a mite. Want to join me? Of course," he said sheepishly, "I ain't no hand with grub."

"I might take some coffee."

Sally swung down, drawing off her gauntlets. She had always seemed a tall girl, but on the ground she came just to his shoulder. Her hair was honey-colored, her eyes gray.

He caught the quick glance of her eyes as she looked around. He saw them hesitate with surprise at the spectacle of flowers blooming near the door. She looked up, and their eyes met.

"Ain't much time to work around," he confessed. "I've sort of been trying to make it look like a home."

"Did you plant the flowers?" she asked curiously.

"Yes, ma'am. My mother was always a great hand for flowers. I like 'em, too, so when I built this cabin, I set some out. The wildflowers, I transplanted."

He poured coffee into a cup and handed it to her. She sipped the hot liquid and looked at him.

"I've been hearing about you," she said.

"From Jingle Bob?"

She nodded. "And some others. Vin Ricker, for one. He hates you."

"Who else?"

"Chen Lee."

"Lee?" Marcy shook his head. "I don't place him."

"He's Chinese, our cook. He seems to know a great deal about you. He thinks you're a fine man. A great fighter, too. He's always talking about some Mullen gang you had trouble with."

"Mullen gang?" He stared. "Why, that was in. . . ." He caught himself. "No, ma'am, I reckon he's mistook. I don't know any Chinese and there ain't no Mullen gang around I know of."

That, he reflected, was no falsehood. The Mullen gang had all fitted very neatly into the boothill he had prepared for them back in Bentown. They definitely weren't around.

"Going to stay here?" she asked, looking at him over her coffee cup, her gray eyes level.

His eyes flashed. "I was fixing to, but I reckon your old man has stopped me by fencing that water hole. He's a hard man, your father."

"It's a hard country." She did not smile. "He's got ideas about it. He drove the Mescaleros out. He wiped out the rustlers. He took this range. He doesn't like the idea of any soft-going, second-run cowhand coming in and taking over."

His head jerked up.

"Soft-going?" he flared. "Second-run? Why, that old billy goat."

Sally turned toward her horse. "Don't tell me. Tell him. If you've nerve enough."

He got up and took the bridle of her horse. His eyes were hard.

"Ma'am," he said, striving to make his voice gentle, "I think you're a mighty fine person, and sure enough pretty, but that father of yours is a rough-riding old buzzard. If it wasn't for that Ricker *hombre*. . . ."

"Afraid?" she taunted, looking down at him.

"No, ma'am," he said quietly. "Only I ain't a killing man. I was raised a Quaker. I don't aim to do no fighting."

"You're in a fighting man's country," she warned him. "And you are cutting in on a fighting man's range."

She turned her gray and started to ride away. Suddenly she reined in and looked back over her shoulder.

"By the way," she said, "there's water up on the rim."

Water up on the rim? What did she mean? He turned his head and stared up at the top of the great cliff, which loomed high overhead into the night. It was fully a mile away, but it seemed almost behind his house.

How could he get up to the rim? Sally had come from that direction. In the morning he would try. In the distance, carried by the still air of night, he heard a cow bawling. It was shut off from the water hole. His six head, starving for water.

Marcy walked out to the corral and threw a

saddle on the moros. He swung into the saddle and rode at a canter toward the water hole.

They heard him coming, and he saw a movement in the shadows by the cottonwoods.

"Hold it!" a voice called. "What do you want?"

"Let that fence down and put them cows through!" Marcy yelled.

There was a harsh laugh. "Sorry, *amigo*. No can do. Only Kenyon cows drink here."

"All right," Marcy snapped. "They are Kenyon cows. I'm giving 'em to him. Let the fence down and let 'em drink. I ain't seeing no animal die just to please an old plug head. Let 'em through."

Then he heard Sally's voice. He saw her sitting her horse beside old Joe Linger, who was her bodyguard, teacher, and friend. An old man who had taught her to ride and to shoot and who had been a scout for the Army at some time in the past.

Sally was speaking, and he heard her say: "Let them through, Texas. If they are our cows, we don't want to have them die on us."

Marcy turned the moros and rode back toward his cabin, a sense of defeat heavy upon him. . . .

He rolled out of his blankets with the sun and, after a quick breakfast, saddled the grayish black horse and started back toward the rim. He kept remembering Sally's words. There is water on the rim. Why had she told him that? What good would water do him if it was way up on the rim?

There must be a way up. By backtracking the girl, he could find it. He was worried about the cattle. The problem of their disappearance kept working into his thoughts. That was another reason for his ride, the major reason. If the cattle were still on his ranch, they were back in the breaks at the foot of the rim.

As he backtracked the girl's horse, he saw cow tracks, more and more of them. Obviously some of his cattle had drifted this way. It puzzled him, yet he had to admit that he knew little of this country.

Scarcely a year before he had come into this range, and, when he arrived, the grass in the lower reaches of the valley was good, and there were mesquite beans. The cattle grew fat. With hotter and dryer weather, they had shown more and more of a tendency to keep to shady hillsides and to the cañons.

The cow tracks scattered out and disappeared. He continued on the girl's trail. He was growing more and more puzzled, for he was in the shadow of the great cliff now, and any trail that mounted it must be frightfully steep. Sally, of course, had grown up in this country on horseback. With her always had been Joe Linger. Old Joe had been one of the first white men to settle in the rim country.

Marcy skirted a clump of piñon and emerged on a little sandy level at the foot of the cliff. This, at one distant time, had been a streambed, a steep stream that originated somewhere back up in the rimrock and flowed down here and deeper into his range.

Then he saw the trail. It was a narrow catwalk of rock that clung to the cliff's edge in a way that made him swallow as he looked at it. The catwalk led up the face of the cliff and back into a deep gash in the face of the rim, a gash invisible from below.

The moros snorted a few times, but true to its mountain blood it took the trail on dainty feet. In an hour Marcy rode out on the rim itself. All was green here, green grass. The foliage on the trees was greener than below. There was every indication of water, but no sign of a cow. Not even a range-bred cow would go up such a trail as Marcy had just ridden.

Following the tracks of the gray, Marcy worked back through the cedar and piñon until he began to hear a muffled roar. Then he rode through the trees and reined in at the edge of a pool that was some twenty feet across. Water flowed into it from a fair-size stream, bubbling over rocks and falling into the pool. There were a number of springs here, and undoubtedly the supply of water was limitless. But where did it go?

Dismounting, Marcy walked down to the edge of the water and knelt on a flat rock and leaned far out.

Brush hung far out over the water at the end of the pool, brush that grew on a rocky ledge no more than three feet above the surface of the water. But beneath that ledge was a black hole at least eight feet long. Water from the pool was pouring into that black hole.

Mac Marcy got up and walked around the pool to the ledge. The brush was very thick, and he had to force his way through. Clinging precariously to a clump of manzanita, he leaned out over the rim of the ledge and tried to peer into the hole. He could see nothing except a black slope of water and that the water fell steeply beyond that slope.

He leaned farther out, felt the manzanita give way slowly, and made a wild clutch at the neighboring brush. Then he plunged into the icy waters of the pool.

He felt himself going down, down, down! He struck out, trying to swim, but the current caught him and swept him into the gaping mouth of the wide black hole under the ledge.

Darkness closed over his head. He felt himself shooting downward. He struck something and felt it give beneath him, and then something hit him a powerful blow on the head. Blackness and icy water closed over him.

Chattering teeth awakened him. He was chilled to the bone and soaking wet. For a moment he lay on hard, smooth rock in darkness, head throbbing, trying to realize what had happened. His feet felt cold. He pulled them up and turned over to a sitting position in a large cave. Only then did he realize his feet had been lying in a pool of water.

Far above he could see a faint glimmer of light, a glimmer feebly reflecting from the black, glistening roar of a fall. He tilted his head back and stared upward through the gloom. That dim light, the hole through which he had come, was at least sixty feet above him!

In falling he had struck some obstruction in the narrow chimney of the water's course, some piece of driftwood or brush insecurely wedged across the hole. It had broken his descent and had saved him.

His matches would be useless. Feeling around the cave floor in the dark, he found some dry tinder that had been lying here for years. He still had his guns, since they had been tied in place with rawhide thongs. He drew one of them, extracted a cartridge, and went to work on it with his hunting knife.

When it was open, he placed it carefully on the rock beside him. Then he cut shavings and crushed dried bark in his hand. Atop this he placed the powder from the open cartridge.

Then he went to work to strike a spark from a rock with the steel back of his knife. There was not the slightest wind here. Despite that, he worked for the better part of an hour before a spark sprang into the powder.

There was a bright burst of flame and the shavings crackled. He added fuel and then straightened up and stepped back to look around.

He stood on a wide ledge in the gloomy, closed cavern at the foot of the fall's first drop, down which he had fallen. The water struck the rock not ten feet away from him. Then it took another steep drop off to the left. He could see by the driftwood that had fallen clear that it was the usual thing for the rushing water to cast all water-borne objects onto this ledge.

The ledge had at one time been deeply gouged and worn by running water. Picking up a torch, Marcy turned and glanced away into the darkness.

There lay the old dry channel, deeply worn and polished by former running water.

At some time in the past, this had been the route of the stream underground. In an earthquake or some breakthrough of the rock, the water had taken the new course.

Thoughtfully Marcy calculated his situation. He was fearful of his predicament. From the first moment of consciousness in that utter darkness, he had been so. There is no fear more universal than the fear of entombment alive, the fear of choking, strangling in utter darkness beyond the reach of help.

Mac Marcy was no fool. He was, he knew, beyond the reach of help. The moros was ground-hitched in a spot where there was plenty of grass and water. The grayish black horse would stay right there.

No one, with the exception of Sally, ever went to the top of the rim. It was highly improbable that she would go again soon. In many cases, weeks would go by without anyone stopping by Marcy's lonely cabin. If he was going to get out of this hole, he would have to do it by his own efforts.

One glance up that fall showed him there was no chance of going back up the way he had come down. Working his way over to the next step downward of the fall, he held out his torch and peered below. All was utter blackness, with only the cold damp of falling water in the air.

Fear was mounting within him now, but he fought it back, forcing himself to be calm and to think carefully. The old dry channel remained a vague hope. But to all appearances it went deeper and deeper into the Stygian blackness of the earth. He put more fuel on his fire and started exploring again. Fortunately the wood he was burning was bone dry and made almost no smoke.

Torch in hand he started down the old dry channel. This had been a watercourse for many, many years. The rock was worn and polished. He had gone no more than sixty feet when the channel divided.

On the left was a black, forbidding hole, scarcely waist high. Down that route most of the water seemed to have gone, as it was worn the deepest.

On the right was an opening almost like a doorway. Marcy stepped over to it and held his torch out. It also was a black hole. He had a sensation of awful depth. Stepping back, he picked up a rock. Leaning out, he dropped it into the hole on the right.

For a long time he listened. Then, somewhere far below, there was a splash. This hole was literally hundreds of feet deep. It would end far below the level of the land on which his cabin stood.

He drew back. Sweat stood out on his forehead, and, when he put his hand to it, his brow felt cold and clammy. He looked at the black waist-high hole on the left and felt fear rise within him as he had never felt it before. He drew back and wet his lips.

His torch was almost burned out. Turning with the last of its light, he retraced his steps to the ledge by the fall.

How long he had been belowground, he didn't

know. He looked up, and there was still a feeble light from above. But it seemed to have grown less. Had night almost come?

Slowly he built a new torch. This was his last chance of escape. It was a chance he had already begun to give up. Of them all, that black hole on the left was least promising, but he must explore it.

He pulled his hat down a little tighter and started back to where the tunnel divided into two holes. His jaw was set grimly. He got down on his hands and knees and edged into the black hole on the left.

Once inside, he found it fell away steeply in a mass of loose boulders. Scrambling over them, he came to a straight, steep fall of at least ten feet. Glancing at the sheer drop, he knew one thing— once down there, he would never get back up.

Holding his torch high, he looked beyond. Nothing but darkness. Behind him there was no hope. He hesitated, and then got down on his hands and knees, lowered himself over the edge, and dropped ten feet.

This time he had to be right, for there was no going back. He walked down a slanting tunnel. It seemed to be growing darker. Glancing up at his torch, he saw it was burning out. In a matter of minutes he would be in total darkness.

He walked faster and faster. Then he broke into a stumbling run, fear rising within him. Something brought him up short, and for a moment he did not see what had caused him to halt in his blind rush. Then hope broke over him like a cold shower of rain.

There on the sand beneath his feet were tiny tracks. He bent over them. A pack rat or some other tiny creature. Getting up, he hurried on, and, seeing a faint glow ahead, he rushed around a bend. There before him was the feeble glow of the fading day. His torch guttered and went out.

He walked on to the cave mouth, trembling in every limb. Mac Marcy was standing in an old watercourse that came out from behind some boulders not two miles from his cabin. He stumbled home and fell into his bunk, almost too tired to undress.

Marcy awakened to a frantic pounding on his door. Staggering erect, he pulled on his boots, yelling out as he did so. Then he drew on his Levi's and shirt and opened the door, buttoning his shirt with one hand.

Sally, her face deathly pale, was standing outside. Beyond her gray mare stood Marcy's moros. At the sight of him the grayish black horse lifted his head and pricked up his ears.

"Oh," Sally gasped. "I thought you were dead . . . drowned."

He stepped over beside her.

"No," he said, "I guess I'm still here. You're pretty scared, ma'am. What's there for you to be scared about?"

"Why," she burst out impatiently, "if you. . . ." She caught herself and stopped abruptly. "After all," she continued coolly, "no one wants to find a friend drowned."

"Ma'am," he said sincerely, "if you get that

wrought up, I'll get myself almost drowned every day."

She stared at him and then smiled. "I think you're a fool," she said. She mounted and turned. "But a nice fool."

Marcy stared after her thoughtfully. Well now, maybe. . . .

He glanced down at his boots. Where they had lain in the pool, there was water stain on them. Also, there was a small green leaf clinging to the rough leather. He stooped and picked it off, wadded it up, and started to throw it away when he was struck by an idea. He unfolded the leaf and studied the veins. Suddenly his face broke into a grin.

"Boy," he said to the moros, "we got us a job to do, even if you do need a rest." He swung into the saddle and rode back toward the watercourse, still grinning.

It was midafternoon when he returned to the cabin and ate a leisurely lunch, still chuckling. Then he mounted again and started for the old water hole that had been fenced by Jingle Bob Kenyon.

When Marcy rounded the bend, he could see that something was wrong. A dozen men were gathered around the water hole. Nearby and astride her gray was Sally.

The men were in serious conference, and they did not notice Marcy's approach. He rode up, leaning on the horn of the saddle, and watched them, smiling.

Suddenly Vin Ricker looked up. His face went

hard. Mac Marcy swung down and strolled up to the fence, leaning casually on a post.

"What's up?"

"The water hole's gone dry!" Kenyon exploded. "Not a drop o' water in it."

Smothering a grin, Marcy rolled a smoke.

"Well," he said philosophically, "the Lord giveth and He taketh away. No doubt it's the curse of the Lord for your greed, Jingle Bob."

Kenyon glared at him suspiciously. "You know somethin' about this?" he demanded. "Man, in this hot weather my cattle will die by the hundreds. Somethin's got to be done."

"Seems to me," Marcy said dryly, "I have heard those words before."

Sally was looking at him over her father's head, her face grave and questioning. But she said nothing, gave no sign of approval or disapproval.

"This here's a man's country," Marcy said seriously. "You fork your own bronc's and you get your own water."

Kenyon flushed. "Marcy, if you know anythin' about this, for goodness sake spill it. My cows will die. Maybe I was too stiff about this, but there's somethin' mighty funny goin' on here. This water hole ain't failed in twenty years."

"Let me handle him," Riker snarled. "I'm just achin' to git my hands on him."

"Don't ache too hard, or you'll git your wish," Marcy drawled, and he crawled through the fence. "All right, Kenyon, we'll talk business," Marcy said to the rancher. "You had me stuck yesterday with my tail in a crack. Now you got yours in one. I cut off your water to teach you a lesson. You're a blamed old highbinder, and it's high time you had some teeth pulled.

"Nobody but me knows how that water's cut off and where. If I don't change it, nobody can. So listen to what I'm saying. I'm going to have all the water I need after this on my own place, but this here hole stays open. No fences.

"This morning, when I went up to cut off your water, I saw some cow tracks. I'm missing a powerful lot of cows. I followed the tracks into a hidden draw and found three hundred of my cattle and about a hundred head of yours, all nicely corralled and ready to be herded across the border.

"While I was looking over the hide-out, I spied Ricker there. John Soley then came riding up with about thirty head of your cattle, and they run 'em in with the rest."

"You're a liar!" Ricker burst out, his face tense, and he dropped into a crouch, his fingers spread.

Marcy was unmoved. "No, I ain't bluffing. You try to prove where you were about nine this morning. And don't go trying to get me into a gunfight. I ain't a-going to draw, and you don't dare shoot me down in front of witnesses. But you take off those guns, and I'll. . . ."

Ricker's face was ugly. "You bet I'll take 'em off! I allus did want a crack at that purty face o' yours."

He stripped off his guns and swung them to Soley in one movement. Then he rushed.

A wicked right swing caught Marcy before he

dropped his gun belt and got his hands up, and it knocked him reeling into the dirt.

Ricker charged, his face livid, trying to kick Marcy with his boots, but Marcy rolled over and got on his feet. He lunged and swung a right that clipped Ricker on the temple. Then Marcy stabbed the rustler with a long left. They started to slug.

Neither had any knowledge of science. Both were raw and tough and hard-bitten. Toe to toe, bloody and bitter, they slugged it out. Ricker, confident and the larger of the two men, rushed in swinging. One of his swings cut Marcy's eye; another started blood gushing from Marcy's nose. Ricker set himself and threw a hard right for Marcy's chin, but the punch missed as Marcy swung one to the body that staggered Ricker.

They came in again, and Marcy's big fist pulped the rustler's lips, smashing him back on his heels. Then Marcy followed it in, swinging with both hands. His breath came in great gasps, but his eyes were blazing. He charged in, following Ricker relentlessly.

Suddenly Marcy's right caught the gunman and knocked him to his knees. Marcy stepped back and let him get up, and then knocked him sliding on his face in the sand. Ricker tried to get up, but he fell back, bloody and beaten.

Swiftly, before the slow-thinking Soley realized what was happening, Marcy spun and grabbed one of his own guns and turned it on this rustler.

"Drop 'em," he snapped. "Unbuckle your belt and step back."

Jingle Bob Kenyon leaned on his saddle horn, chewing his pipe stem thoughtfully.

"What," he drawled, "would you have done if he drawed his gun?"

Marcy looked up, surprised. "Why, I'd have killed him, of course." He glanced over at Sally, and then looked back at Kenyon. "Before we get off the subject," he said, "we finish our deal. I'll turn your water back into this hole . . . I got it stopped up away back inside the mountain . . . but, as I said, the hole stays open to anybody. Also"—Marcy's face colored a little—"I'm marrying Sally."

"You're what?" Kenyon glared, and then jerked around to look at his daughter.

Sally's eyes were bright. "You heard him, Father," she replied coolly. "I'm taking back with me those six steers he gave you so he can get them to water."

Marcy was looking at Kenyon when suddenly Marcy grinned.

"I reckon," he said, "you had your lesson. Sally and me have got a lot of talking to do."

Marcy swung aboard the moros, and he and Sally started off together.

Jingle Bob Kenyon stared after them, grim humor in his eyes.

"I wonder," he said, "what he would have done if Ricker had drawed?"

Old Joe Linger grinned and looked over at Kenyon from under his bushy brows. "Jest what he said. He'd've kilt him. That's Quaker John McMarcy, the *hombre* that wiped out the Mullen gang single-handed. He jest don't like to fight, that's all."

"It sure does beat all," Kenyon said thoughtfully. "The trouble a man has to go to git him a good son-in-law these days."

West of the Tularosa

I

The dead man had gone out fighting. Scarcely more than a boy, and a dandy in dress, he had been man enough when the showdown came.

Propped against the fireplace stones, legs stretched before him, loose fingers still touching the butt of his .45 Colt, he had smoked it out to a bloody, battle-stained finish. Evidence of it lay all about him. Whoever killed him had spent time, effort, and blood to do it.

As they closed in for the pay-off at least one man had died on the threshold.

The fight that ended here had begun elsewhere. From the looks of it this cabin had been long deserted, and the dead man's spurs were bloodstained. At least one of his wounds showed evidence of being much older than the others. A crude attempt had been made to stop the bleeding.

Baldy Jackson, one of the Tumbling K riders who found the body, dropped to his knees and picked up the dead man's Colt.

"Empty," he said. "He fought 'em until his guns were empty, an' then they killed him."

"Is he still warm?" McQueen asked. "I think I can smell powder smoke."

"He ain't been an hour dead, I'd guess. Wonder what the fuss was about?"

"It worries me"—McQueen looked around—"considering our situation." He glanced at Bud Fox and Kim Sartain, who appeared in the doorway. "What's out there?"

"At least one of their boys rode away still losing blood. By the look of things this lad didn't go out alone. He took somebody with him." Sartain was rolling a smoke. "No feed in the shed, but that horse out there carries a mighty fine saddle."

"Isn't this the place we're headed for?" Fox asked. "It looks like the place described."

Sartain's head came up. "Somebody comin'," he said. "Riders, an' quite a passel of them."

Sartain flattened against the end of the fireplace and Fox knelt behind a windowsill. Ward McQueen planted his stalwart frame in the doorway, waiting. "This isn't so good. We're going to be found with a dead man, just killed."

There were a half dozen riders in the approaching group, led by a stocky man on a gray horse and a tall, oldish man wearing a badge.

They drew up sharply on seeing the horses and McQueen. The short man stared at McQueen, visibly upset by his presence. "Who're you? And what are you doin' here?"

"I'll ask the same question," McQueen spoke casually. "This is Firebox range, isn't it?"

"I know that." The stocky man's tone was testy. "I ought to. I own the Firebox."

"Do you now?" Ward McQueen's reply was gentle, inquiring. "Might be a question about that. Ever hear of Tom McCracken?"

"Of course. He used to own the Firebox."

"That's right, and he sold it to Ruth Kermitt of the Tumbling K. I'm Ward McQueen, her foreman. I've come to take possession."

His reply was totally unexpected, and the stocky man was obviously astonished. His surprise held him momentarily speechless, and then he burst out angrily.

"That's impossible! I'm holdin' notes against young Jimmy McCracken. He was the old man's heir, an' Jimmy signed the place over to me to pay up."

"As of when?" Ward asked.

His thoughts were already leaping ahead, reading sign along the trail they must follow. Obviously something was very wrong, but he was sure that Ruth's deed, a copy of which he carried with him, would be dated earlier than whatever this man had. Moreover, he knew that the dead man lying behind him was that same Jimmy McCracken.

"That's neither here nor there. Get off my land or be drove off."

"Take it easy, Webb." The sheriff spoke for the first time. "This man may have a just claim. If Tom McCracken sold out before he died, your paper isn't worth two hoots."

That this had occurred to Webb was obvious, and that he did not like it was apparent. Had the sheriff not been present, Ward was sure, there would have been a shooting. As yet, they did not know he was not alone, as none of the Tumbling K men had shown themselves.

"Sheriff," McQueen said, "my outfit rode in here about fifteen minutes ago, and we found a dead man in this cabin. Looks like he lost a running fight with several men, and, when his ammunition gave out, they killed him."

"Or you shot him," Webb said.

Ward did not move from the door. He was a big man, brown from sun and wind, lean and muscular. He wore two guns.

"I shot nobody." His tone was level, even. "Sheriff, I'm Ward McQueen. My boss bought this place from McCracken for cash money. The deed was delivered to her, and the whole transaction was recorded in the courts. All that remained was for us to take possession, which we have done."

He paused. "The man who is dead inside is unknown to me, but I'm making a guess he's Jimmy McCracken. Whoever killed him wanted him dead mighty bad. There were quite a few of them, and Jimmy did some good shooting. One thing you might look for is a couple of wounded men, or somebody else who turns up dead."

The sheriff dismounted. "I'll look around, McQueen. My name's Foster, Bill Foster." He waved a hand to the stocky cattleman. "This is Neal Webb, owner of the Runnin' W."

Ward McQueen stepped aside to admit the sheriff, and, as he did so, Kim Sartain showed up at the corner of the house, having stepped through a window to the outside. Kim Sartain was said to be as good with his guns as McQueen.

Foster squatted beside the body. "Yeah, this is young Jimmy, all right. Looks like he put up quite a scrap."

"He was game," McQueen said. He indicated the older wound. "He'd been shot somewhere and rode in here, riding for his life. Look at the spurs. He tried to get where there was help but didn't make it."

Foster studied the several wounds and the empty cartridge cases. McQueen told him of the hard-ridden mustang, but the sheriff wanted to see for himself. Watching the old man, McQueen felt renewed confidence. The lawman was careful and shrewd, taking nothing for granted, accepting no man's unsupported word. That McQueen and his men were in a bad position was obvious.

Neal Webb was obviously a cattleman of some local importance. The Tumbling K riders were not only strangers but they had been found with the body.

Webb was alert and aware. He had swiftly catalogued the Tumbling K riders as a tough lot, if pushed. McQueen he did not know, but the foreman wore his guns with the ease of long practice. Few men carried two guns, most of them from the Texas border country. Nobody he knew of used both at once; the second gun was insurance, but it spoke of a man prepared for trouble.

Webb scowled irritably. The set-up had been so perfect. The old man dead, the gambling debts, and the bill of sale. All that remained was to . . . and then this outfit appeared with what was apparently a legitimate claim. Who would ever dream the old man would sell out. But how had the sale been arranged? There might still be a way, short of violence.

What would Silas Hutch say? And Ren Oliver? It angered Webb to realize he had failed, after all his promises. Yet who could have foreseen this? It had all appeared so simple, but who could have believed that youngster would put up a fight like he did? He had been a laughing, friendly youngster, showing no sense of responsibility, no steadiness of purpose. He had been inclined to side-step trouble rather than face it, so the whole affair had looked simple enough.

One thing after another had gone wrong. First, the ambush failed. The kid got through it alive and then had made a running fight of it. Why he had headed for this place Webb could not guess, unless he had known the Tumbling K outfit was to be here.

Two of Webb's best men were dead and three wounded, and he would have to keep them out of sight until they were well again. Quickly he decided the line cabin on Dry Legget would be the best hide-out.

Foster came from the woods, his face serious.

"McQueen, you'd better ride along to town with me. I found sign that six or seven men were in this fight, and several were killed or hurt. This requires investigation."

"You mean I'm under arrest?"

"No such thing. Only you'll be asked questions. We'll check your deed an' prob'ly have to get your boss up here. We're goin' to get to the bottom of this."

"One thing, Foster, before we go. I'd like you to check our guns. Nobody among us has fired a shot for days. I'd like you to know that."

You could have switched guns," Webb suggested.

McQueen ignored him. "Kim, why don't you fork your bronc' and ride along with us? Baldy, you and Bud stay here and let nobody come around unless it's the sheriff or one of us. Got it?"

"You bet." Jackson spat a stream of tobacco juice at an ant. "Nobody'll come around, believe me."

Neal Webb kept his mouth shut but he watched irritably. McQueen was thinking of everything, but, as Webb watched the body of young Mc-Cracken being tied over a saddle, he had an idea. Jimmy had been well liked around town, so if the story got around that McQueen was his killer, there might be no need for a trial or even a preliminary hearing. It was too bad Foster was so stiff-necked.

Kim Sartain did not ride with the group. With his Winchester across his saddlebow he kept off to the flank or well back in the rear where the whole group could be watched. Sheriff Foster noted this, and his frosty old eyes glinted with amused appreciation.

"What's he doin' back there?" Webb demanded. "Make him ride up front, Sheriff."

Foster smiled. "He can ride where he wants. He don't make me nervous, Webb. What's eatin' you?"

The town of Pelona for which they were riding

faced the wide plains from the mouth of Cottonwood Cañon, and faced them without pretensions. The settlement, dwarfed by the bulk of the mountain behind it, was a supply point for cattlemen, a stage stop, and a source of attraction for cowhands to whom Santa Fe and El Paso were faraway dream cities.

In Pelona, with its four saloons, livery stable, and five stores, Si Hutch, who owned Hutch's Emporium, was king.

He was a little old man, grizzled, with a stubble of beard and a continually cranky mood. Beneath that superficial aspect he was utterly vicious, without an iota of mercy for anything human or animal.

Gifted in squeezing the last drop of money or labor from those who owed him, he thirsted for wealth with the same lust that others reserved for whiskey or women. Moreover, although few realized it, he was cruel as an Apache and completely depraved. One of the few who realized the depth of his depravity was his strong right-hand man, Ren Oliver.

Oliver was an educated man and for the first twenty-five years of his life had lived in the East. Twice, once in New York and again in Philadelphia, he had been guilty of killing. In neither case had it been proved, and in only one case had he been questioned. In both cases he had killed to cover his thieving, but finally he got in too deep and, realizing his guilt could be proved, he skipped town.

In St. Louis he shot a man over a card game. Two months later he knifed a man in New Orleans, then drifted West, acquiring gun skills as he traveled. Since boyhood his career had been a combination of cruelty and dishonesty, but not until he met Si Hutch had he made it pay. Behind his cool, somewhat cynical expression few people saw the killer.

He was not liked in Pelona. Neither was he disliked. He had killed two men in gun battles since arriving in town, but both seemed to have been fair, stand-up matches. He was rarely seen with Si Hutch, for despite the small population they had been able to keep their cooperation a secret. Only Neal Webb, another string to Hutch's bow, understood the connection. One of the factors that aided Hutch in ruling the Pelona area was that his control was exercised without being obvious. Certain of his enemies had died, by means unknown to either Ren Oliver or Neal Webb.

The instrument of these deaths was unknown, and for that reason Si Hutch was doubly feared.

When Sheriff Foster rode into town with Webb and McQueen, Si Hutch was among the first to know. His eyes tightened with vindictive fury. That damned Webb! Couldn't he do anything right? His own connection with the crimes well covered, he could afford to sit back and await developments.

Ward McQueen had been doing some serious thinking on the ride into town. The negotiations between Ruth Kermitt and old Tom McCracken had been completed almost four months ago. McCracken had stayed on at the Firebox even after the title was transferred and was to have managed it for another six months. His sudden death ended all that.

Webb had said he owned the ranch by virtue of young Jimmy's signing it over to pay a gambling debt. This was impossible, for Jimmy had known of the sale and had been present during the negotiations. That, then, was an obvious falsehood. Neal Webb had made an effort to obtain control of the ranch, and Jimmy McCracken had been killed to prevent his doing anything about it.

The attempt to seize control of the ranch argued a sure and careful mind, and a ruthless one. Somehow he did not see Webb in that rôle, although Webb was undoubtedly a part of the operation. Still, what did he know? Pelona was a strange town and he was a stranger. Such towns were apt to be loyal to their own against any outsider. He must walk on cat feet, careful to see where he stepped. Whoever was in charge did not hesitate to kill, or hesitate to lose his own men in the process.

Sheriff Foster seemed like an honest man, but how independent was he? In such towns there were always factions who controlled, and elected officials were often only tools to be used.

Faced with trickery and double-dealing as well as such violence, what could he do? When Ruth arrived from the Tumbling K in Nevada, there would be no doubt that she owned the Firebox and that Jimmy had known of it. That would place the killing of young Jimmy McCracken at Neal Webb's door.

Ren Oliver was on the walk in front of the Bat Cave Saloon when they tied up before the sheriff's office. He had never seen either McQueen or Sartain before but knew them instantly for what they were, gunfighters, and probably good.

McQueen saw the tall man in the gray suit standing on the boardwalk. Something in the way he carried himself seemed to speak of what he was. As he watched, Oliver turned in at the Emporium. Ward finished tying his roan and went into the sheriff's office.

Nothing new developed from the talk in the office of the sheriff, nor in the hearing that followed. Young Jimmy McCracken had been slain by persons unknown after a considerable chase. The evidence seemed to establish that several men had been involved in the chase, some of whom had been killed or wounded by McCracken.

Ward McQueen gave his own evidence and listened as the others told what they knew or what the tracks seemed to indicate. As he listened, he heard whispering behind him, and he was well aware that talk was going around. After all, he and the Tumbling K riders were strangers. What talk he could overhear was suspicion of his whole outfit.

Neal Webb had a bunch of tough men around him and he was belligerent. When telling what he knew, he did all he could to throw suspicion on the Tumbling K. However, from what McQueen could gather, all of Webb's riders were present and accounted for. If Webb had been one of those involved in the killing of McCracken, it must have been with other men than his own.

After the inquest McQueen found himself standing beside the sheriff. "What kind of a country is this, Sheriff? Do you have much trouble?"

"Less than you'd expect. Webb's outfit is the biggest, but his boys don't come in often. When they want to have a blowout, they ride down to Alma. They do some drinkin' now an' again, but they don't r'ar up lookin' for trouble."

"Many small outfits?"

"Dozen or so. The Firebox will be the largest if you run cows on all of it." Foster studied him. "Do you know the range limits of the Firebox?"

"We figure to run stock from the Apache to Rip-Roaring Mesa and Crosby Creek, south to Dillon Mountain, and up to a line due east from there to the Apache."

"That's a big piece of country but it is all Firebox range. There are a few nesters squatted in Bear Cañon, and they look like a tough outfit, but they've given me no trouble."

"Miss Kermitt holds deeds on twelve pieces of land," Ward explained. "Those twelve pieces control most of the water on that range, and most of the easy passes. We want no trouble, but we'll run cattle on range we're entitled to."

"That's fair enough. Watch your step around Bear Cañon. Those boys are a mean lot."

II

Kim Sartain was somewhere around town but McQueen was not worried. The gunslinging *segundo* of the Tumbling K was perfectly capable of taking care of himself, and in the meanwhile Ward had business of his own to take care of. He glanced up and down the street, studying the stores. Two of them appeared better stocked than the others. One was Hutch's Emporium, a large store apparently stocked to the doors with everything a rancher could want. The other stores were smaller but were freshly painted and looked neat.

McQueen walked along to the Emporium. A small man with a graying beard looked up at him as he came to the counter. It was an old-fashioned counter, curved inward on the front to accommodate women shoppers who wore hoopskirts.

"Howdy there! Stranger in town?"

"Tumbling K. We've taken over the Firebox, and we'll need supplies."

Hutch nodded agreeably. "Glad to help. The Firebox, hey? Had a ruckus out there, I hear."

"Nothing much." Ward walked along, studying the goods on the shelves and stacked on tables. He was also curious about the man behind the counter. He seemed genial enough, but his eyes were steel-bright and glassy. He was quick-moving and obviously energetic.

"Troublin' place, the Firebox. Old McCracken seemed to make it pay but nobody else ever done it. You reckon you'll stay?"

"We'll stay."

McQueen ordered swiftly and surely, but not all they would need. There were other stores in town, and he preferred to test the water before he got in too deep. The Firebox would need to spend a lot of money locally and he wanted to scatter it around. Hutch made no comment until he ordered a quantity of .44-caliber ammunition.

"That's a lot of shootin'. You expectin' a war?"

"War? Nothing like that, but we're used to wars. Jimmy McCracken was killed for some reason by some right vicious folks. If they come back, we wouldn't want them to feel unwelcome."

The door opened and Neal Webb walked in. He strode swiftly to the counter and was about to speak when he recognized McQueen. He gulped back his words, whatever they might have been.

"Howdy. Reckon you got off pretty easy."

McQueen took his time about replying. "Webb, the Tumbling K is in this country to stay. You might as well get used to us and accept the situation. Then we can have peace between us and get on with raising and marketing cattle. We want no trouble, but we're ready if it comes. We did business with Mc-Cracken and I couldn't have found a finer man. His son seemed cut from the same pattern.

"They didn't belong to my outfit, so I'm dropping this right here. If it had been one of my men, I'd back-trail the killers until I found where they came from. Then I'd hunt their boss and I'd stay with him until he was hanged, which is what he deserves."

Behind McQueen's back Hutch gestured, and the hot remarks Webb might have made were stifled. Puzzled, McQueen noticed the change and the sudden shift of Webb's eyes. Finishing his order, he stepped into the street.

As he left, a gray-haired, impatient-seeming man brushed by him. "Neal," he burst out, "where's that no-account Bemis? He was due over to my place with that horse he borried. I need that paint the worst way."

"Forget it," Webb said. "I'll see he gets back to you."

"But I want to see Bemis. He owes me money."

Ward McQueen let the door close behind him and glanced across the street. A girl with red-gold hair was sweeping the boardwalk there. She made a pretty picture and he crossed the street.

As he stepped up on the walk, she glanced up. Her expression changed as she saw him. Her glance was the swiftly measuring one of a pretty girl who sees a stranger, attractive and possibly unmarried. She smiled.

"You must be one of that new outfit the town's talking about. The Tumbling K, isn't it?"

"It is." He shoved his hat back on his head. *Kim should see this girl*, he thought. *She's lovely.* "I'm the foreman."

She glanced across the street toward Hutch's store. "Started buying from Hutch? Like him?"

"I don't know him. Do you run this store?"

"I do, and I like it. What's more I almost make money with it. Of course Hutch gets most of the business. I've had no trouble with him, so far."

He glanced at her. Did that mean she expected trouble? Or that Hutch was inclined to cause trouble for competitors?

"I'm new here so I thought I'd scatter my business until I find out where I get the best service." He smiled. "I want to order a few things."

A big man was coming up the walk, a very big man, and Ward McQueen sensed trouble in the man's purposeful stride. He was taking in the whole walk, and he was bareheaded. His worn boots were run down at the heels and his faded shirt was open halfway down his chest for lack of buttons. His ponderous fists swung at the ends of powerfully muscled arms, and his eyes darkened savagely as he saw Ward McQueen.

"Watch yourself," the girl warned. "That's Flagg Warneke."

The big man towered above McQueen. When he came to a stop in front of Ward, his chin was on a level with Ward's eyebrows and he seemed as wide as a barn door.

"Are you McQueen? Well, I'm Flagg Warneke, from Bear Cañon. I hear you aim to run us nesters off your range. Is that right?"

"I haven't made up my mind yet," Ward replied. "When I do, I'll come to see you."

"Oh, you haven't made up your mind yet? Well, see that you don't. And stay away from Bear Cañon! That place belongs to us, an', if you come huntin' trouble, you'll get it."

Coolly Ward McQueen turned his back on the giant. "Why not show me what stock you have?" he suggested to the girl. "I. . . ."

A huge hand clamped on his shoulder and spun him around. "When I talk to you, face me!" Warneke roared.

As the big hand spun him around, Ward McQueen threw a roundhouse right to the chin that knocked the big man floundering against the post of the overhang. Instantly Ward moved in, driving a wicked right to the body, and then swinging both hands to the head.

The man went to his knees and McQueen stepped back. Then, as if realizing for the first time that he had been struck, Warneke came off the walk with a lunge. He swung his right but Ward went inside, punching with both hands. The big man soaked up punishment like a sponge takes water, and he came back, punching with remarkable speed for such a big man.

A blow caught McQueen on the jaw and he crashed against the side of the store, his head ringing. Warneke followed up on the punch, but he was too eager for the kill and missed.

Ward stepped in, smashing his head against the big man's chin, and then punching with both hands to the body. His head buzzed and his mouth had a taste of blood. The big man clubbed at his kidneys and tried to knee him, but Ward slid away and looped a punch that split Warneke's ear and showered Ward with blood.

Warneke staggered but, recovering, came back, his eyes blazing with fury. When Warneke threw a punch, Ward went under it and grabbed the big man by the knees, upending him. The big man hit the walk on his shoulder blades with a crash that raised dust, but he came up fast, landing a staggering right to Ward's head. Ward countered with a left, and then crossed a right to the jaw. The big man went to his haunches.

A crowd had gathered and the air was filled with shouted encouragement to one or the other. Ward's shirt was torn, and, when he stepped back to let Warneke get up again, his breath was coming in great gasps. The sheer power and strength of the big man was amazing. He had never hit a man so hard and had him still coming.

McQueen, no stranger to rough-and-tumble fighting, moved in, circling a little. Warneke, cautious now, was aware he was in a fight. Before, his battles had always ended quickly; this was different. McQueen stabbed a left to the mouth, feinted, and did it again. He feinted again, but this time he whipped a looping uppercut to the body that made Warneke's mouth fall open. The big man swung a ponderous blow that fell short and McQueen circled him warily. The speed was gone from the Bear Cañon man now, and McQueen only sought a quick way to end it.

McQueen, oblivious of the crowd, moved in warily. Warneke, hurt though he was, was as dangerous as a cornered grizzly. McQueen's greatest advantage had been that Warneke had been used to quick victories and had not expected anything like what had happened. Also, McQueen had landed the first blow and followed it up before the bigger man could get set. He stalked him now, and then feinted suddenly and threw a high hard one to the chin. Warneke was coming in when the blow landed.

For an instant he stiffened, and then fell forward to the walk and lay still.

McQueen stepped back to the wall and let his eyes sweep the faces of the crowd. For the first time he saw Sartain standing in front of the store, his thumbs hooked in his belt, watching the people gathered about.

Nearest the porch was a tall man in a gray suit, a man he had observed before when he first rode into town.

"That was quite a scrap," said the man in gray. "My congratulations. If there is ever anything I can do, just come to me. My name is Ren Oliver."

"Thanks."

Ward McQueen picked up his fallen hat, and then tentatively he worked his fingers. Nothing was broken but his hands were stiff and sore from the pounding. He gave Sartain a half smile. "Looks like we've picked a tough job. That was a Bear Cañon nester."

"Yeah." Kim gave him a wry look. "Wonder who put him up to it?"

"You think it was planned?"

"Think about it. You've made no decision on

Bear Cañon. You ain't even seen the place or its people, but he had the idea you were going to run them off. And how did he know where you were and who you were? I think somebody pointed you out."

"That's only if somebody has it in for him, or for us."

Sartain's smile was cynical. "You don't think they have? You should have seen how green Webb turned when you said you had title to the Firebox. If the sheriff hadn't been there, he'd have tried to kill you. And why was the sheriff there? That's another thing we'd better find out."

McQueen nodded. "You're right, Kim. While you're around, keep your eyes and ears open for a man named Bemis. You won't see him, I think, but find out what you can about him."

"Bemis? What do you know about him?"

"Darned little." McQueen touched his cheek with gentle fingers where a large red, raw spot had resulted from Warneke's fist. "Only he ain't around, and he should be."

Sartain walked off down the street and the crowd drifted slowly away, reluctant to leave the scene. McQueen hitched his guns into place and straightened his clothes. He glanced around and saw a sign: Clarity's Store.

The girl had come back into her doorway, and he glanced at her. "Are you Clarity?"

"I am. The first name is Sharon and I'm Irish. Did they call you McQueen?"

"They did. And the first name is Ward."

He stepped into the store, anxious to get away

from the curious eyes. The store was more sparsely stocked than Hutch's much larger store, but the stock gave evidence of careful selection and a discriminating taste. There were many things a Western store did not normally stock.

"I have a wash basin," she suggested. "I think you'd better take a look at yourself in a mirror."

"I will," he said, grinning a little, "but I'd rather not." He glanced around again. "Do you stock shirts by any chance? Man-size shirts?"

She looked at him critically. "I do, and I believe I have one that would fit you."

She indicated the door to the wash basin, and then went among the stacks of goods on the shelves behind the counter.

A glance in the mirror and he saw what she meant. His face was battered and bloody, his hair mussed. He could do little about the battering, but the blood he could wash away, and he did so. The back door opened on a small area surrounded by a high fence. It was shaded by several old elms and a cottonwood or two, and in the less shaded part there were flowers. He washed his face, holding compresses on his swollen cheekbones and lip. Then he combed his hair.

Sharon Clarity came with a shirt. It was a dark blue shirt with two pockets. He stripped off the rags of his other shirt and donned the new one and dusted off his hat.

She gave him a quick look and a smile when he emerged, saying: "It's an improvement, anyway." She folded some other shirts and returned them to the shelves.

He paid for the shirt she had provided, and she said: "You know what you've done, don't you? You've whipped the toughest man in Bear Cañon. Whipped him in a stand-up fight. Nobody has ever done that, and nobody has even come close. Nobody has even tried for a long time."

She paused, frowning a little. "It puzzles me a little. Warneke isn't usually quarrelsome. That's the first time I ever saw him start a fight."

"Somebody may have given him an idea. I hadn't had time to even think about Bear Cañon. I haven't even ridden over the ranch, and yet he had the idea we were about to run the nesters off."

She looked at him appraisingly, at the wide shoulders, the narrow hips. There was power in every line of him, a power she had just seen unleashed with utter savagery. Having grown up with four brawling brothers, she knew something about men. This one had fought coolly, skillfully. "You've started something, you know. That Bear Cañon outfit is tough. Even Neal Webb's boys fight shy of them."

"Webb has a tough outfit?"

"You've seen some of them. There are two or three known killers in the bunch. Why he keeps them, I couldn't say."

"Like Bemis, for example?"

"You know Harve Bemis? He's one of them, but not the worst by a long shot. The worst ones are Overlin and Bine."

These were names he knew. Bine he had never seen, but he knew a good deal about him, as did any cattleman along the border country of Texas.

An occasional outlaw and suspected rustler, he had run with the Youngers in Missouri before riding south to Texas.

Overlin was a Montana gun hand known around Bannock and Alder Gulch, but he had ridden the cattle trails from Texas several times and was a skilled cowhand, as well. McQueen had seen him in Abilene and at Doan's Crossing. On that occasion he himself had killed an outlaw who was trying to cut the herd with which McQueen was riding. The fact that such men rode with Webb made the situation serious.

He purchased several items, and then hired a man with a wagon to freight the stuff to the Firebox. Kim Sartain was loitering in front of the saloon when McQueen came down to get his horse.

"Bemis ain't around," he confided, "an' it's got folks wonderin' because he usually plays poker at the Bat Cave Saloon. Nobody's seen him around for several days." He paused. "I didn't ask. I just listened."

III

For three days the Firebox was unmolested, and in those three days much was accomplished. The shake roof needed fixing, and some fences had to be repaired. Baldy had that job, and, when he finished, he stood back and looked it over with satisfaction. "Bud, that there's an elephant-proof fence."

"Elephant-proof? You mean an elephant couldn't get past that fence? You're off your trail."

"Of course it's elephant-proof. You don't see any elephants in there, do you?"

Bud Fox just looked at him and rode away.

All hands were in the saddle from ten to twelve hours a day. The cattle were more numerous than expected, especially the younger stuff. Several times McQueen cut trails made by groups of riders, most of them several days old. Late on the afternoon of the third day he rode down the steep slope to the bottom of a small cañon near the eastern end of the Dillons and found blood on the grass.

The stain was old and dark but unmistakably blood. He walked his horse around, looking for sign. He found a leaf with blood on it, then another. The blood had come from someone riding a horse, a horse that toed in slightly. Following the trail he came to where several other horsemen had joined the wounded man. One of the other horses was obviously a led horse.

Men had been wounded in the fight with McCracken. Could these be the same? If so, where were they going? He rode on over the Dillons and off what was accepted as Firebox range. He had crossed a saddle to get into this narrow cañon, but farther along it seemed to open into a wider one. He pushed on, his Winchester in his hands.

The buckskin he rode was a mountain horse accustomed to rough travel. Moreover, it was fast and had stamina, the sort of horse a man needed when riding into trouble. The country into which he now ventured was unknown to him, wild and rough. The cañon down which he rode opened into a wider valley that tightened up into another deep, narrow cañon. Before him was a small stream. The riders had turned downcañon.

It was dusk and shadows gathered in the cañons, only a faint red glow from the setting sun crested the rim of the cañon. Towering black walls lifted about him, and on the rocky edge across the way a dead, lightning-blasted pine pointed a warning finger from the cliff. The narrow valley was deep in the mystery of darkness, and the only sound that came from the stream was a faint rustling. Then wind sighed in the junipers and the buckskin stopped, head up, ears pricked.

"*Ssh*," he whispered, putting a warning hand on the buckskin's neck. "Take it easy, boy. Take it easy now."

The horse stepped forward, seeming almost to walk on tiptoe. This was the Box, one of the deepest cañons in the area. McCracken had spoken of it during their discussions that led to his sale of the ranch.

Suddenly he glimpsed a faint light on the rock wall. Speaking softly to the buckskin, he slid from the saddle, leaving his rifle in the scabbard.

Careful to allow no jingle of spurs, he felt his way along the sandy bottom. Rounding a shoulder of rock, he saw a small campfire and the moving shadow of a man in a wide hat. Crouching near a bush, he saw that shadow replaced by another, a man with a bald head.

In the silence of the cañon, where sounds were magnified, he heard a voice. "Feelin' better, Bemis? We'll make it to Dry Leggett tomorrow."

The reply was huskier, the tone complaining. "What's the boss keepin' us so far away for? Why didn't he have us to the Runnin' W? This hole I got in me is no joke."

"You got to stay under cover. We're not even suspected, an' we won't be if we play it smart."

His eyes picked out three men lying near the fire, covered with blankets, one with a bandaged head. One of those who was on his feet was preparing a meal. From the distance he could just make out their faces, the shape of their shoulders, and of the two on their feet the way they moved. Soon he might be fighting these men, and he wanted to know them on sight. The man in the wide hat turned suddenly toward him.

Hansen Bine!

Never before had he seen the man but the grapevine of the trails carried accurate descriptions of such men and of places as well. Gunfighters were much discussed, more than prize fighters or baseball players, even more than racehorses or buckers.

Bine was known for his lean, wiry body, the white scar on his chin, and his unnaturally long, thin fingers. "What's the matter, Bine?" Bemis asked.

"Somethin' around. I can feel it."

"Cat, maybe. Lots of big ones in these cañons. I saw one fightin' a bear one time. A black bear. No lion in his right mind would tackle a grizzly."

Bine looked again into the night, and then crossed to the fire and seated himself. "Who d'you reckon those riders were who went to the cabin after we left? I saw them headed right for it."

"The boss, maybe. He was supposed to show up with the sheriff."

There was silence except for the crackling of the fire, only barely discernible at the distance. The flames played shadow games on the rock wall. Then Bemis spoke: "I don't like it, Hans. I don't like it at all. I been shot before, but this one's bad. I need some care. I need a doctor."

"Take it easy, Bemis. You'll get there, all in good time."

"I don't like it. Sure, he doesn't want nobody to know, but I don't want to die, either."

Talk died down as the men sat up to eat, and Ward drew carefully back and walked across the sand to his horse. He swung into the saddle and turned the animal, but, as the buckskin lined out to go back along the cañon, its hoof clicked on stone.

He had believed himself far enough away not to be heard, but from behind him he heard a startled exclamation, and Ward put the horse into a lope in the darkness. From behind him there was a challenge, and then a rifle shot, but he was not worried. The shot would have been fired on chance, as Ward knew he could not be seen and there was no straight shot possible in the cañon.

He rode swiftly, so swiftly that he realized he had missed his turn and was following a route up a cañon strange to him. The bulk of the Dillons arose on his right instead of ahead or on his left as they should be. By the stars he could see that the cañon up which he now rode was running east and west and he was headed west. Behind him he heard sounds of pursuit but doubted they would follow far.

The riding was dangerous, as the cañon was a litter of boulders and the trunks of dead trees. A branch cañon opened and he rode into it, his face into a light wind. He heard no further sounds of pursuit and was pleased, wanting no gun battle in these narrow, rock-filled cañons where a ricochet could so easily kill or wound a man. He saw the vague gleam of water and rode his horse into a small mountain stream. Following the stream for what he guessed was close to a mile, he found his way out of the stream to a rocky shelf. A long time later he came upon a trail and the shape of some mountains he recognized.

As he rode, he considered what he had heard. Harve Bemis, as he suspected, had been one of those who attacked Jimmy McCracken. More than likely Bine had been there as well. That, even without what else he knew of Neal Webb, placed the attack squarely on Webb's shoulders.

With Jimmy McCracken slain and a forged bill of sale, Webb would have been sure nothing could block his claim to the Firebox range.

So what would he do now? Relinquish his attempt to seize the Firebox and let the killing go for nothing? All McQueen's experience told him otherwise. Webb would seek some other way to advance his claim, and he would seek every opportunity to blacken the reputation of the Tumbling K riders.

The men he had seen in the cañon were headed for Dry Leggett. Where was that? What was it? That he must find out; also he must have a talk with Sheriff Bill Foster. Ruth Kermitt would not like this. She did not like trouble, and yet those who worked for her always seemed to be fighting to protect her interests. Of late she had refused to admit there might be occasions when fighting could not be avoided. She had yet to learn that in order to have peace both sides must want it equally. One side cannot make peace; they can only surrender. Ward McQueen knew of a dozen cases where one side had agreed to lay down their arms if allowed to leave peacefully. In every case of which he knew, the ones who surrendered their arms were promptly massacred.

He had been in love with Ruth since their first

meeting, and they had talked of marriage. Several times they had been on the verge of it but something always intervened. Was it altogether accident? Or was one or both of them hesitating? Marriage would be new for each, yet he had always been a freely roving man, going where he willed, living as he wished.

He shook such thoughts from his head. This was no time for personal considerations. He was a ranch foreman with a job to do, a job that might prove both difficult and dangerous. He must put the Firebox on a paying basis.

Their Nevada ranch was still the home ranch, but Ruth had bought land in other states, in Arizona and New Mexico as well as Utah, and she had traded profitably in cattle. One of the reasons for his hesitation, if he was hesitating, was because Ruth Kermitt was so wealthy. He himself had done much to create that wealth and to keep what she had gained. From the time when he had saved her herd in Nevada he had worked untiringly. He knew cattle, horses, and men. He also knew range conditions. The Tumbling K range fattened hundreds of white-faced cattle. The Firebox, farther south and subject to different weather conditions, could provide a cushion against disaster on the northern range. She had bought, on his advice, for a bargain price. Old Tom and young Jimmy had planned to return to a property they owned in Wyoming. As Tom had known Ruth's father, he offered her a first chance.

On Ward's advice she had purchased land around

water holes, insuring her of water so they would control much more land than they owned.

It was almost daybreak when McQueen rolled into his bunk in the Firebox bunkhouse. Sartain opened an eye and glanced at him curiously. Then he went back to sleep. Kim asked no questions and offered no comments but missed little.

IV

Baldy Jackson was putting breakfast together when McQueen awakened. He sat up on his bunk and called out to Baldy in the next room. "Better get busy and muck this place out," Ward suggested. "Ruth . . . Miss Kermitt . . . may be down before long."

"Ain't I got enough to do? Cookin' for you hungry coyotes, buildin' fence, an' mixin' 'dobe? This place is good enough for a bunch of thistle-chinned cowhands."

"You heard me," McQueen said cheerfully. "And while you're at it, pick out a cabin site for the boss. One with a view. She will want a place of her own."

"Better set up an' eat. You missed your supper."

"Where's the boys? Aren't they eating?"

"They et an' cleared out hours ago." Baldy glanced at him. "What happened last night? Run into somethin'?"

"Yes, I did." He splashed water on his face and hands. "I came upon a camp of five men, three of them wounded. They were headed for a place called Dry Leggett."

"Cañon west of Plaza."

"Plaza?"

"Kind of settlement, mostly Mexicans. Good people. A few 'dobes, a couple of stores, and a saloon or two."

"How well do you know this country, Baldy?"

Jackson gave him a wry look. "Pretty well. I punched cows for the SU south of here, and rode into Plaza more times than I can recall. Been over around Socorro. Back in the old days I used to hole up back in the hills from time to time."

Baldy was a good cowhand and a good cook, but in his younger years he had ridden the outlaw trail until time brought wisdom. Too many of his old pals had wound up at the end of a rope.

"Maybe you can tell me where I was last night. I think I was over around that cañon they used to call the Box." He described the country and Baldy listened, sipping coffee. "Uhn-huh," he said finally, "that cañon you hit after crossing the Dillons must have been Devil. You probably found them holed up in the Box or right below it. Leavin', you must have missed Devil Cañon and wound up on the south fork of the Frisco. Then you come up the trail along the Centerfire and home."

Racing hoofs interrupted. McQueen put down his cup as Bud Fox came through the door.

"Ward, that herd we gathered in Turkey Park is gone! Sartain trailed 'em toward Apache Mountain."

"Wait'll I get my horse." Baldy jerked off his apron.

"You stay here," McQueen told him. "Get down

that Sharps and be ready. Somebody may have
done this just to get us away from the cabin. Anyway, I've a good idea who is responsible."

Riding swiftly, Fox led him to the tracks. Kim
Sartain had followed after the herd. The trail skirted
a deep cañon, following an intermittent stream into
the bed of the Apache, and then crossed the creek
into the rough country beyond.

Suddenly McQueen drew up, listening. Ahead
of them they heard cattle lowing. Kim came down
from the rocks.

"Right up ahead. Four of the wildest, roughest-
lookin' hands I've seen in years."

"Let's go," McQueen said. Touching spurs to his
horse as he plunged through the brush and hit the
flat land at a dead run with the other two riders
spreading widely behind him. The movements of
the cattle killed the sound of their charge until
they were almost up to the herd. Then one of the
rustlers turned and slapped a hand for his six-
shooter. McQueen's gun leaped to his hand and he
chopped it down, firing as it came level. The rush
of his horse was too fast for accurate shooting and
his bullet clipped the outlaw's horse across the
back of the neck. It dropped in its tracks, spilling
its rider. Ward charged into the rustler, knocking
him sprawling, almost under the hoofs of the
buckskin.

Swinging wide, McQueen saw that Sartain had
downed his man, but the other two were converg-
ing on Bud Fox. Both swung away when they saw
Kim and McQueen closing in. One of them swung
a gun on Kim and Kim's gun roared. The man

toppled from the saddle and the last man quickly lifted his hands.

He was a thin, hard-featured man with narrow, cruel eyes. His hair was uncut, his jaws unshaved. His clothing was ragged. There was nothing wrong with his gun; it was new and well-kept.

Now his face, despite its hardness, wore a look of shock. His eyes went from McQueen to Sartain to Fox. "You boys shoot mighty straight but you'll wish you never seen the day!"

Fox took his rope from the saddletree. "He's a rustler, Ward, caught in the act, an' there's plenty of good trees."

"Now, look . . . !" the man protested, suddenly frightened.

"What gave you the idea you could run off our stock?" Ward asked.

"Nothin'. The stock was in good shape." He looked suddenly at McQueen who still wore the marks of battle. "You're the gent who whipped Flagg. He'll kill you for that, if not for this. You won't live a week."

"Bud, tie this man to his saddle and tie him tight. We'll take him into town for the law to handle. Then we'll visit Bear Cañon."

"You'll do what?" their prisoner sneered. "Why, you fool! Flagg will kill you! The whole bunch will!"

"No," Ward assured him, "they will not. If they'd left my stock alone, they could have stayed. Now they will get out or be burned out. That's the message I'm taking to them."

"Wait a minute." The man's eyes were restless.

Suddenly his arrogance was gone and he was almost pleading. "Lay off Bear Cañon. This was none o' their doin', anyway."

"You're talking," Ward said, and waited.

"Neal Webb put us up to it. Promised us fifteen bucks a head for every bit of your stock we throwed into the Sand Flats beyond Apache."

"Will you say that to a judge?"

His face paled. "If you'll protect me. That Webb outfit, they kill too easy to suit me."

When they rode down the street of Pelona to the sheriff's office, the town sprawled lazily in the sunshine. By the time they reached the sheriff's office, nearly fifty men had crowded around. Foster met them at the door, his shrewd old eyes going from McQueen to the rustler.

"Well, Chalk"—He spat.—"looks like you run into the wrong crowd." His eyes shifted to McQueen. "What's he done?"

"Rustled a herd of Firebox stock."

"Him alone?"

"There were four of them. The other three were in no shape to bring back. They won't be talking. This one will."

A man at the edge of the crowd turned swiftly and hurried away. McQueen's eyes followed him. He went up the walk to the Emporium. A moment later Ren Oliver emerged and started toward them.

"Who were the others, Chalk? Were they from Bear Cañon?"

"Only me." Chalk's eyes were haunted. "Let's get inside."

"Hang him!" somebody yelled. "Hang the rustler!"

The voice was loud. Another took it up, then still another. McQueen turned to see who was shouting. Somebody else shouted: "Why waste time? Shoot him!"

The shot came simultaneously with the words, and Ward McQueen saw the prisoner fall, a hole between his eyes.

"Who did that?" Ward's contempt and anger were obvious. "Anybody who would shoot an unarmed man with his hands tied is too low-down to live."

The crowd stirred but nobody even looked around. Those who might know were too frightened to speak. On the edge of the crowd Ren Oliver stood with several others who had drawn together. "I didn't see anybody fire, McQueen, but wasn't the man a rustler? Hasn't the state been saved a trial?"

"He was also a witness who was ready to testify that Neal Webb put him up to the rustling and was paying for the cattle."

Startled, people in the crowd began to back away, and from the fringes of the crowd they began to disappear into stores or up and down the street. There seemed to be no Webb riders present, but Kim Sartain, sitting his horse back from the crowd, a hand on his gun butt, was watching. He had come up too late to see the shooting.

"Webb won't like that, McQueen," Ren Oliver said. "I speak only from friendship."

"Webb knows where to find me. And tell him this time it won't be a kid he's killing."

Sheriff Foster chewed on the stub of his cigar. His blue eyes had been watchful. "That's some charge you've made, McQueen. Can you back it up?"

Ward indicated the dead man. "There's my witness. He told me Webb put him up to it, and that Bear Cañon wasn't involved. As for the rest of it. . . ."

He repeated the story of the tracks he had followed, of the men holed up in the Box.

"You think they went on to Dry Leggett?" Foster asked.

"That was what I heard them say, but they might have changed their minds. Bemis was among the wounded and he was worried. He had a wound and wanted care." Then he added: "Bine did most of the talking."

Ward McQueen tied his horse in front of Sharon Clarity's store, where there was shade. With Sartain at his side he crossed to the Bat Cave.

The saloon was a long, rather narrow room with a potbellied stove at either end and a bar that extended two-thirds the room's length. There were a roulette table and several card tables.

A hard-eyed, bald-headed bartender leaned thick forearms on the bar, and three men loafed there, each with a drink. At the tables several men played cards. They glanced up as the Tumbling K men entered, then resumed their game.

McQueen ordered two beers and glanced at Ren Oliver, who sat in one of the card games. Had Oliver been only a bystander? Or had he fired the shot that killed Chalk?

Oliver glanced up and smiled. "Care to join our game?" McQueen shook his head. He would have enjoyed playing cards with Oliver, for there are few better ways to study a man than to play cards with him. Yet he was in no mood for cards, and he hadn't the time. He had started something with his comments about Webb. Now he had to prove his case.

He finished his beer, and then, followed by Sartain, he returned to the street. Ren Oliver watched them go, then cashed in, and left the game. When he entered the Emporium, Hutch glared at him.

"Get rid of him!" Hutch said. "Get rid of him now!"

Oliver nodded. "Got any ideas?"

Hutch's eyes were mean. "You'd botch the job. Leave it to me!"

"You?" Oliver was incredulous.

Hutch looked at him over his steel-rimmed glasses. Ren Oliver, who had known many hard men, remembered only one such pair of eyes. They were the eyes of a big swamp rattler he had killed as a boy. He remembered how those eyes had stared into his. He felt a chill.

"To me," Hutch repeated.

V

It was dark when Ward McQueen, trailed by Kim and Bud Fox, reached the scattered, makeshift cabins in Bear Cañon. It was a small settlement, and he had heard much about it in the short time he had been around. The few women were hard-eyed slatterns as tough as their men. Rumor had it they lived by rustling and horse thieving or worse.

"Bud," McQueen said, "stay with the horses. When we leave, we may have to leave fast. Be ready, and, when you hear me yell, come a-running."

Followed by Kim, he walked toward the long bunkhouse that housed most of the men. Peering through a window, he saw but two men, one playing solitaire, the other mending a belt. The room was lighted by lanterns. Nearby was another house, and, peering in, they saw a short bar and a half dozen men sitting around. One of them was Flagg Warneke.

Ward McQueen stepped to the door and opened it. He stepped in, Kim following, moving quickly left against the log wall.

Flagg saw them first. He was tipped back in his

chair and he let the legs down carefully, poised for trouble.

"What d' you want?" he demanded. "What're you doin' here?"

All eyes were on them. Two men, four guns, against six men and eight guns. There were others around town.

"This morning Chalk and some other riders ran off some of our cows. We had trouble and three men got killed. I told Chalk, if he told me who was involved, I'd not ride down here. He didn't much want me to come to Bear Cañon, and to tell you the truth I hadn't been planning on coming down here. Chalk started to talk, and somebody killed him."

"Killed him? Killed Chalk? Who did it?"

"You make your own guess. Who was afraid of what he might say? Who stood to lose if he did talk?"

They absorbed this in silence, and then a fat-faced man at the end of the table asked: "Those fellers with Chalk? You say you killed them?"

"They chose to fight."

"How many did you lose?"

"We lost nobody. There were three of us, four of them. They just didn't make out so good."

"What're you here for?" Flagg demanded.

"Two things. To see if you have any idea about who killed Chalk and to give you some advice. Stay away from Firebox cattle."

Silence hung heavily in the room. Flagg's face was still swollen from the beating he had taken and the cuts had only begun to heal. His eyes were hard as he stared at McQueen.

"We'll figure out our own answers to the first question. As to the second, we've no use for Fire- box cows. As for you and that feller with you . . . get out."

McQueen made no move. "Remember, friend, Bear Cañon is on Firebox range. What you may not know is that Firebox owns that land, every inch of it. You stay if Firebox lets you, and right now the Firebox is me. Behave yourselves and you'll not be bothered, but next time there will be no warning. We'll come with guns and fire."

He reached for the latch with his left hand, and, as the door opened, Flagg said: "I put my mark on you, anyway."

McQueen laughed. "And you're wearing some of mine. Regardless of how things work out, Flagg, it was a good fight and you're a tough man to whip."

He opened the door, and Kim Sartain stepped out and quickly away. He followed. Yet they had taken no more than three steps when the door burst open and the fat-faced man lunged out, holding a shotgun in both hands. He threw the shotgun to his shoulder. As one man, Ward and Kim drew and fired. The fat-faced man's shotgun sagged in his hands and he backed up slowly and sat down.

Men rushed from the bunkhouse and Kim shot a man with a buffalo gun. Ward shot through the open door at the hanging lantern. It fell, spewing oil and flame. In an instant the room was afire.

Men and women rushed from the other buildings and the two backed to their horses, where Bud awaited them on the rim of the firelight.

Several men grabbed a heavy wagon by the tongue and wheeled it away from the fire. Others got behind to shove. Of Flagg, McQueen saw nothing.

As the three rode away, they glanced back at the mounting flames. The saloon was on fire, as well as the bunkhouse.

"Think this will move them out?" Kim asked.

"I've no idea. I'm no hand for the sort of thing. Not burning folks out. They'd no right there, and that's deeded land, as I told them. They may have believed it to be government land. If they'd acted halfway decent, I'd have paid them no mind."

"There's no good in that crowd," Kim said.

"Maybe not, but Flagg fought a good fight. He had me worried there, for a spell."

"He didn't get into this fight."

"No, and I think he'd have acted all right. I think he has judgment, which I can't say for that fat-faced gent. He just went hog wild."

Baldy Jackson was pacing the yard and muttering when they rode in. "Durn it all! You fellers ride away with your shootin' irons on. Then we hear nothin' of you! Where've you been?"

"What do you mean *we?*" Kim said. "Since when have you become more than one?"

"He was including me, I think." Sharon Clarity got up from the chair where she had been sitting. "But I've only been here a few minutes. I came to warn you."

"To warn us?"

"To warn you, Mister McQueen. Sheriff Foster is coming for you. He will arrest you for killing Neal Webb."

"For what?" Ward swung down from his horse and trailed the reins. "What happened to Webb?"

"He was found dead on the trail not fifteen minutes after you left town. He had been shot in the back."

Neal Webb killed. Ward McQueen sat down in one of the porch chairs. By whom, and for what? Ward McQueen knew what Western men thought of a back-shooter. That was a hanging offense before any jury one could get, but more often a lynch mob would handle such cases before the law got around to it.

Kim Sartain had been with him, but he would be considered a prejudiced witness.

"Pour me some coffee, Baldy," he suggested. He glanced over at Sharon Clarity. "And thanks." He hesitated. "I hope your riding to warn me won't make enemies for you."

"Nobody knew," she replied cheerfully. "Anyway, I think you and the Tumbling K are good for this country. Things were getting kind of one-sided around here."

"Neal Webb killed?" Ward mused. "I wonder what that means? I'd sort of thought he was behind all the trouble, but this makes me wonder."

"It does, doesn't it?" Sharon said. "Almost as if he was killed purely to implicate you."

He glanced at her. "That's a shrewd observation.

Any idea who would want to do a thing like that? After all, my trouble was with Webb."

She did not reply. She got to her feet. "My father used to box," she said. "Back in the old country he was considered quite good. They had a rule in boxing. I've heard him quote it. It was 'protect yourself at all times.' I am going back to town, but I think you should be very, very careful. And you'd better go. Foster will have about thirty riders in that posse. You'd better start moving."

"I've done nothing. I'll wait for them to come.

She went to her horse. "When you get thirty men together," Sharon said, "you get all kinds. You have to consider their motives, Mister McQueen."

"Kim, ride along with Miss Clarity, will you? See that she gets safely home."

"Yes, sir." Kim had been tired. Suddenly he was no longer so. "But what about that posse?"

"There'll be no trouble. Take good care of Miss Clarity. She is a very bright young woman."

In Pelona, Oliver went to the Bat Cave and seated himself at the card table. The saloon was empty save for himself and the bartender, a man with whom he was not particularly friendly, but the cards were there and he gathered them up and began to shuffle. He always thought better with cards in his hands. He carefully laid out a game of solitaire, but his mind was not on the cards.

He was both puzzled and worried. For some years now he had considered himself both an astute and a wise young man. He made his living with his adept fingers and his skill at outguessing men with cards. He knew all the methods of cheating and was a skilled card mechanic, but he rarely used such methods. He had a great memory for cards and the odds against filling any hand. He won consistently without resorting to questionable methods. He rarely won big. The show-off sort of thing that attracted attention he did not want. He played every day, and, when he lost, it was only small amounts. The sums he won were slightly larger. Sometimes he merely broke even, but over the months he was a clear and distinct winner. At a time when a cowhand was pulling down $30 to $40 a month, and a clerk in a store might work for as little as half that, Ren Oliver could pull down $200 to $250 without attracting undue attention. When a professional gambler starts winning big pots, he becomes suspect.

Even Hutch did not realize how well he was doing, and Hutch was providing him with a small income for rendering various services not to be discussed. Over the past year Ren Oliver had built up a nice road stake, something to take with him when he left, for he was well aware that few things last, and many difficulties could be avoided by forming no lasting attachments and keeping a fast horse.

Now Ren Oliver was disturbed. Neal Webb had been killed. By whom was a question, but an even larger question was why.

It disturbed him that he did not know. The obvious answer was that he had been killed by Ward McQueen, but Oliver did not buy that, not for a minute. McQueen might kill Webb in a gun battle, but he would not shoot him in the back.

Moreover, there had been no confrontation between them. The other answer was that Neal had outlived his usefulness and was killed to implicate McQueen.

But who had actually killed him?

It disturbed Oliver that he did not know. Obviously Hutch was behind it, but who had done the killing? One by one he considered the various men available and could place none of them in the right position. This worried him for another reason. He had considered himself close to Hutch, yet he now realized that, like Webb, when he ceased to be useful, he might be killed. He was merely a pawn in another man's game.

For a man of Oliver's disposition and inclinations it was not a pleasant thought. He did not mind others believing he was a pawn, but he wished to be in control so he could use those who believed they were using him. Now he had the uncomfortable sensation that too much was happening of which he was not aware and that any moment he might be sacrificed.

He had no illusions about himself. He was without scruples. It was his attitude that human life was cheap, and like most men engaged in crime he regarded people as sheep to be sheared. He was cold and callous and had always been so.

Outwardly he was friendly and ingratiating. He went out of his way to do favors for people even while holding them in contempt. You never knew when such people might appear on a jury.

For the same reason he had allied himself with Hutch.

It was unsettling to realize there was someone more cunning than he himself. He knew Hutch was hunching over his community like a huge spider of insatiable appetite. Within that community he was considered to be something of a skinflint but nothing more. Men came and went from his store because, after all, it was the town's leading emporium, as its name implied. That all those people might not be buying was not considered. Oliver believed Hutch hired his killing done, but who did he hire?

Bine, of course, but who else? When Oliver looked over his shoulder, he wanted to know who he was looking for. The fact that there was an unsuspected actor in the play worried him.

He had the uncomfortable feeling that Neal Webb had been killed not only to implicate McQueen but to serve as a warning to him and perhaps to others. A warning that nobody was indispensable.

Oliver shuffled the cards again, ran up a couple of hands with swiftness and skill, then dealt them, taking several off the bottom with smoothness and ease, yet his mind was roving and alert.

Would Hutch manage it? He had never yet, so far as Oliver knew, encountered such a man as McQueen. Not that Oliver had any great opinion of McQueen. He was typically a cowman, honest, tough, and hard-working. That he was good with a gun was obvious, and that *segundo* of his, Kim Sartain, was probably almost as good.

Did McQueen have brains? How would he fare

against Hutch, particularly when, as Oliver believed, McQueen did not know who his enemy was.

Hutch had planted the Webb killing squarely on McQueen. The timing had been good and there would be witnesses, Oliver was sure. Trust the old man for that.

He watched Sheriff Foster leave town with his posse, and knew that several of the men in that posse were owned by Hutch. If the slightest excuse was offered, they were to shoot to kill. He knew their instructions as if he had heard them himself.

The door opened and a squat, powerful man entered, his hair shaggy and untrimmed. His square, granite-like face was clean-shaved. He had gimlet eyes that flickered with a steely glint. He wore two guns, one in a holster, the other thrust into his waistband. This was Overlin, the Montana gunman.

"Where's Foster goin'?"

"After McQueen, for the Webb killing."

"Webb? Is he dead?"

Oliver nodded. "Out on the trail." Overlin could have done it. So could Hansen Bine, but, so far as anyone knew, Bine was with the wounded men at Dry Leggett. "There's a witness to swear he did it."

"He might have," Overlin commented, "only I don't believe it. I've heard of McQueen. Made quite a reputation along the cattle trails and in the mining camps. He's no bargain."

"He's only one man. Maybe he'll be your dish one day."

"Or yours," Overlin agreed. "Only I'd like him, myself."

Ren Oliver remembered McQueen and said: "You can have him." He could not understand such men as Overlin. The man was good with a gun, but why would he go out of his way to match skills with a man he believed might be just as good? Overlin had to be the best. He had to know he was best.

Oliver believed he was faster with a gun than either Bine or Overlin but he was a sure-thing man. He had pride in his skill but preferred to take no chances. He would enjoy killing Ward McQueen if he could do so at no risk to himself.

A horse loped into the street, the rider waving at someone out of sight. It was Sharon Clarity. Now where had she been at this hour of the night?

"See you around," he said to Overlin, and went into the night.

He dug a cigar from his pocket and lighted it. Sharon Clarity's horse had been hard-ridden.

VI

Ward McQueen was working beside Baldy Jackson, building a pole corral, when the sheriff and the posse rode into the ranch yard. McQueen continued to place a pole in position and lash it there with rawhide. Then he glanced around at the posse.

"Howdy, Foster. Looks like you're here on business."

"I've come for you, McQueen. There's witnesses says you shot Neal Webb, shot him in the back."

McQueen kept his hands in sight, moving carefully not to give any false impressions. His eyes caught the slight lift to the muzzle of a Winchester and he eyed the man behind it, staring at him until the man's eyes shifted and he swallowed.

"All you had to do was send for me, Sheriff. I'd have come right in. No need for all this crowd." He paused. "And you know, Sheriff, I'd never shoot any man in the back. What would be the point? Webb was never supposed to be good with a gun, and, if I wanted him killed that bad, all I'd have to do would be to pick a fight with him in town. Webb's temper had a short fuse, and killing him would have been no trick."

"That may be so, but you've got to come in with me and answer charges. There will have to be a trial."

"We'll see. Maybe I can prove I was elsewhere."

"By one of your own men?" The man who spoke had a sallow face and buckteeth. "We'd not be likely to believe them."

"By others, then? Kim Sartain was with me, however, and, if you believe he's a liar, why don't you tell him so?"

"We want no trouble, McQueen. Saddle a horse and come along." Foster's eyes went to the cabin. Was there somebody inside the window?

"I'll come on one condition. That I keep my guns. If I can't keep 'em, you'll have to take me and you'll have some empty saddles on your way back to town."

Foster was angry. "Don't give me any trouble, McQueen! I said, saddle your horse!"

"Sheriff, I've no quarrel with you. You're just doing your duty and I want to cooperate, but you've some men riding with you who would like to make a target of my back. Let me keep my guns and I'll go quiet. In case you'd like to know there are two men behind you with Winchesters. They will be riding along behind us."

Sheriff Foster studied McQueen. Inwardly he was pleased. This McQueen was a hardcase but a good man. Shoot a man in the back? It was preposterous. Especially Neal Webb.

"All right," he said, "saddle up."

"My horse is ready, Foster. A little bird told me you were coming, and my horse has been ready."

It was a black he was riding this day, a good mountain horse with bottom and speed. As he mounted and settled into the saddle, he glanced at the man who had lifted his rifle.

"Just so everybody will understand. Two of my boys are going to follow us into town. Either one of them could empty a Winchester into the palm of your hand at three hundred yards."

He sat solidly and well in the saddle, his black Frisco jeans tight over his thighs, his broad chest and shoulders filling the dark gray shirt. His gun belts were studded with silver, the walnut grips worn from use. "All right, Sheriff, let's go to town."

He rode alongside of Foster, but his thoughts were riding ahead, trying to foresee what would happen in town, and asking himself the question again: why kill Neal Webb? Who wanted him dead?

He had believed Webb the ringleader, the cause of his troubles. Most ranchers wanted more range, most of them wanted water, so the attempt to seize the Firebox came as no surprise. In fact, he would have been surprised had it not been claimed. Good grass was precious, and, whenever anybody moved or died, there was always someone ready to move in. The difference here was that McCracken had been a shrewd man and he had purchased the land around the various water holes, as well as the trails into and out of the range he used. The claim on Firebox range by McCracken was well established.

Webb, he was beginning to suspect, had been a mere pawn in the game, and had been disposed of when his usefulness ceased to be. But Webb's dying had implicated Ward McQueen and apparently somebody had decided to have him killed, either in capturing him or in the ride to town. A posse member could shoot him, claiming McQueen had made a move to escape.

Behind this there had to be a shrewd and careful brain. If there were witnesses to something that had not happened, his supposed murder of Neal Webb, then somebody had provided them.

Who? Why?

The Firebox was valuable range. The only other large ranch was Webb's Running W, and who was Webb's heir? Or did he himself own that ranch?

The Bear Cañon crowd? It wasn't their sort of thing. They might drygulch him, steal his horses or cattle, or even burn him out, but the Webb killing was more involved. Anyway, Webb had left the Bear Cañon crowd alone.

Would Sharon Clarity know? She was a handsome, self-reliant girl, yet something about her disturbed him. Why had she ridden out to warn him the sheriff was coming? Had she believed he would run?

Liking for him? Dislike of somebody else? Women's thinking was not part of his expertise. He had trouble reading their brands. Did she know who plotted against him? Did she herself hope to seize the Firebox when the shooting was over?

Who now owned the Running W? This he must discover. If that unknown owner also owned the Firebox, he would control all the range around Pelona and the town as well. It made a neat, compact package and a base from which one might move in any direction.

Ruth Kermitt owned the Firebox now, and Ruth had no heirs. Ward McQueen was suddenly glad his boss was not among those present.

Pelona's main street was crowded with rigs and saddle horses when they rode in. Word had spread swiftly, and the people of the range country— the few scattered small ranchers, farmers, and gardeners—had come in, eager for any kind of a show. All had known Neal Webb, at least by sight. Many had not liked him, but he was one of their own. This Ward McQueen was a stranger and, some said, a killer. The general attitude was that he was a bad man.

A few, as always, had misgivings. Their doubts increased when they saw him ride into town sitting his horse beside the sheriff. He was not in irons. He still wore his guns. Evidently Foster trusted him. Western people, accustomed to sizing up a man by his looks, decided he didn't look like somebody who needed to drygulch anybody. It was more likely Webb would try to drygulch him!

Some of those who came to see drifted up between the buildings into the street. Among these was Bud Fox, with his narrow-brimmed gray hat and his long, lean body, looking like an overgrown schoolboy. The pistol on his belt was man-size, however, and so was the Winchester he carried.

Kim Sartain, young, handsome, and full of deviltry, they recognized at once. They had seen his sort before. There was something about him that always drew a smile, not of amusement but of liking. They knew the guns on his belt were not there for show, but the West had many a young man like

him, good cowhands, great riders, always filled
with humor. They knew his type. The guns added
another dimension, but they understood that, too.

The pattern was quickly made plain. The preliminary hearing was already set and the court was
waiting. McQueen glanced at the sheriff. "Looks
like a railroading, Foster. Are you in this?"

"No, but I've nothing against the law movin'
fast. It usually does around here."

"When who is to get the brunt of it? Who's the
boss around town, Foster? Especially when they
move so fast I have no time to find witnesses."

"You know as much as I do." Foster was testy.
"Move ahead!"

"If I'd been around as long as you have, I'd know
plenty."

The judge was a sour-faced old man who Mc-
Queen had seen about town. Legal procedures on
the frontier were inclined to be haphazard, although
often they moved not only swiftly but efficiently
as well. The old Spanish courts had often func-
tioned very well indeed, but the Anglos were inclined to follow their own procedures. McQueen
was surprised to find that the prosecuting attor-
ney, or the man acting as such, Ren Oliver, was
said to have practiced law back in Missouri.

Sartain sat down beside McQueen. "They've got
you cornered, Ward. Want me to take us out of
here?"

"It's a kangaroo court, but let's see what happens. I don't want to appeal to Judge Colt unless
we have to."

The first witness was a cowhand Ward had seen

riding with Webb's men. He swore he had dropped behind Webb to shoot a wild turkey. He lost the turkey in the brush and was riding to catch up when he heard a shot and saw McQueen duck into the brush. He declared McQueen had fired from behind Webb.

McQueen asked: "You sure it was me?"

"I was sworn in, wasn't I?"

"What time was it?"

"About five o'clock of the evenin'."

"Webb comes from over east of town when he comes to Pelona, doesn't he? From the Running W? And you say you saw me between you and Webb?"

"I sure did." The cowboy was emphatic, but he glanced at Oliver, uncertainly.

"Then"—McQueen was smiling—"you were lookin' right into the setting sun when you saw somebody take a shot at Webb? And you were able to recognize me?" As the crowd in the courtroom stirred, McQueen turned to the judge. "Your Honor, I doubt if this man could recognize his own sister under those circumstances. I think he should be given a chance to do it this evening. It's nice and clear like it was the other night and the sun will be setting before long. I think his evidence should be accepted if he can distinguish four out of five men he knows under the conditions he's talking about."

The judge hesitated and Oliver objected.

"Seems fair enough!" A voice spoke from the crowd, and there was a murmured assent.

The judge rapped for silence. "Motion denied! Proceed!"

Behind him McQueen was aware of changing

sentiment. Western courtrooms, with some excep-
tions, were notoriously lax in their procedure, and
there were those who had an interest in keeping
them so. Crowds, however, were partisan and re-
sentful of authority. The frontier bred freedom,
but with it a strong sense of fair play and an impatience with formalities. Most Western men wanted
to get the matter settled and get back to their work.
Most of the men and women present had ridden
over that road at that time of the evening, and they
saw immediately the point of his argument.

There was a stir behind them, and, turning,
they saw Flagg Warneke shoving his way through
the crowd and then down the aisle.

"Judge, I'm a witness. I want to be sworn in."

The judge's eyes flickered to Oliver, who nodded quickly. Warneke still bore the marks of
McQueen's fists, and his evidence could only be
damning.

Warneke was sworn in and took the stand. Kim
muttered irritably but Ward waited, watching the
big man.

"You have evidence to offer?" the judge asked.

"You bet I have," Warneke stated violently. "I
don't know who killed Neal Webb, but I know
Ward McQueen didn't do it."

Ren Oliver's face tightened with anger. He
glanced swiftly toward a far corner of the room, a
glance that held appeal and something more. Mc-
Queen caught the glance and sat a little straighter.
The room behind him was seething, and the judge
was rapping for order.

"What do you mean by that statement?" Oliver

demanded. He advanced threateningly toward Warneke. "Be careful what you say and, remember, you are under oath."

"I remember. McQueen whipped me that evenin', like you all know. He whipped me good but he whipped me fair. Nobody else ever done it or could do it. I was mad as a steer with a busted horn. I figured, all right, he whipped me with his hands but I'd be durned if he could do it with a six-shooter, so I follered him, watchin' my chance. I was goin' to face him, right there in the trail, an' kill him.

" 'Bout the head of Squirrel Springs Cañon I was closin' in on him when a turkey flew up. That there McQueen, he slaps leather and downs that turkey with one shot! You hear me? One shot on the wing, an' he drawed so fast I never seen his hand move."

Flagg Warneke wiped the sweat from his brow with the back of his hand. "My ma, she never raised any foolish children. Anybody who could draw that fast and shoot that straight was too good for anybody around here, and I wanted no part of him.

"Important thing is, McQueen was never out of my sight from the time he left town headin' west an' away from where Webb was killed until he reached Squirrel Springs Cañon, and that's a rough fifteen miles, the way he rode. It was right at dusk when he shot that turkey, so he never even seen Webb, let alone killed him."

Ren Oliver swore under his breath. The crowd was shifting; many were getting up to leave. He glanced again toward the corner of the room and waited while the judge pounded for order.

Oliver attacked Warneke's testimony but could not shake the man. Finally, angered, he demanded: "Did McQueen pay you to tell this story?"

Warneke's face turned ugly. "Pay me? Nobody lives who could pay me for my oath. I've rustled a few head of stock, and so has every man of you in this courtroom if the truth be known. I'd shoot a man if he crossed me, but by the eternal my oath ain't for sale to no man.

"I got no use for McQueen. He burned us out over in Bear Cañon. He shot friends of mine, but he shot 'em face-to-face when they were shootin' at him. The man I'd like to find is the one who killed Chalk. Shot him off his horse to keep him from tellin' that Webb put them up to rustlin' Firebox stock."

Ward McQueen got to his feet. "Judge, I'd like this case to be dismissed. You've no case against me."

The judge looked at Ren Oliver, who shrugged and turned away.

"Dismissed!"

The judge arose from his bench and stepped down off the platform. Ward McQueen turned swiftly and looked toward the corner of the room where Oliver's eyes had been constantly turning. The chair was empty.

People were crowding toward the door. McQueen's eyes searched their faces. Only one turned to look back. It was Silas Hutch.

McQueen pushed his way through the crowd to Flagg Warneke. The big man saw him coming and faced him, eyes hard.

"Warneke," McQueen said, "I'd be proud to shake the hand of an honest man!"

The giant's brow puckered and he hesitated, his eyes searching McQueen's features for some hint of a smirk or a smile. There was none. Slowly the big man put his hand out and they shook.

"What are your plans? I could use a hand on the Firebox."

"I'm a rustler, McQueen. You've heard me admit it. You'd still hire me?"

"You had every reason to lie a few minutes ago, and I think a man who values his word that much would ride for the brand if he took a job. You just tell me you'll play it straight and rustle no more cattle while you're working for me and you've got a job."

"You've hired a man, McQueen. And you have my word."

As the big man walked away, Sartain asked: "You think he'll stand hitched?"

"He will. Warneke has one thing on which he prides himself. One thing out of his whole shabby, busted-up life that means anything, and that's his word. He'll stick, and we can trust him."

VII

Tough as Ward McQueen felt himself to be, when he rode back to the ranch, he was sagging in the saddle. For days he had little sleep and had been eating only occasionally. Now, suddenly, it was hitting him. He was tired, and he was half asleep in the saddle when they rode into the yard at the Tumbling K's Firebox.

Lights in the cabin were ablaze and a buckboard stood near the barn. Stepping down from the saddle, he handed the reins to Kim. No words were necessary.

He stepped up on the low porch and opened the door.

Ruth Kermitt stood with her back to the fireplace, where a small fire blazed. Even at this time of the year, at that altitude, a fire was needed.

She was tall, with a beautifully slim but rounded body that clothes could only accentuate. Her eyes were large and dark, her hair almost black. She was completely lovely.

"Ward." She came to him quickly. "You're back."

"And you're here." He was pleased but worried, also. "You drove all the way from the ranch?"

"McGowan drove. Shorty rode along, too. He said it was to protect me, but I think he had an idea you were in trouble. Naturally, if that were the case, Shorty would have to be here."

"Ruth," he told her, "I'm glad to have you here. Glad for me, but I don't think you should have come. There is trouble, and I'm not sure what we've gotten into."

He explained, adding: "You know as well as I do that where there's good grass, there will always be somebody who wants it, and what some of them haven't grasped is that we are not moving in on range. We own the water holes and the sources of water."

He put his hands on her shoulders. "All that can wait." He drew her to him. His lips stopped hers and he felt her body strain toward him and her lips melt softly against his. He held her there, his lips finding their way to her cheek, her ears, and her throat. After a few minutes she drew back, breathless.

"Ward! Wait!"

He stepped back and she looked up at him.

"Ward? Tell me. Has there been trouble? Baldy said you were in court, that you might have to go on trial."

"That part is settled, but there's more to come, I'm afraid."

"Who is it, Ward? What's been happening?"

"That's just the trouble." He was worried. "Ruth,

I don't know who it is, and there may be a joker in the deck that I'm not even aware of."

She went to the stove for the coffeepot. "Sit down and tell me about it."

"The ranch is a good one. Excellent grass, good water supply, and, if we don't try to graze too heavy, we should have good grass for years. McCracken handled it well and he developed some springs, put in a few spreader dams to keep the run-off on the land, but he wanted to sell, and I am beginning to understand why."

"What about the trouble? Has it been shooting trouble?"

"It has, but it started before we got here." He told her about the killing of McCracken, then his own brush with rustlers, and the fight with Flagg Warneke and the killing of Chalk, Flagg Warneke's brother, before he could talk. And then the killing of Neal Webb.

"Then he wasn't the one?"

"Ruth, I believe Webb had played out his usefulness for whoever is behind this, who deliberately had Webb killed, with the hope of implicating me. He'd have done it, too, but for Warneke."

"He must be a strange man."

"Warneke's a big man. You'll see him. He's also a violent man, but at heart he's a decent fellow. His word is his pride. I think he's going to shape up into quite a man. Some men get off on the wrong foot simply because there doesn't seem any other way to go. Without him, I think that Bear Cañon outfit will drift out and move away. I doubt if they will try to rebuild what was destroyed."

"Ward, we've been over this before. I hate all this violence. The fighting, the killing. It's awful. My own brother was killed. But you know all that. It was you who pulled us out of that."

"I don't like it, either, but it is growing less, Ruth, less with each year. The old days are almost gone. What we have here is somebody who is utterly ruthless, someone who has no respect for human life at all. You're inclined to find good in everybody, but in some people there just isn't any. Whoever is behind this, and I've a hunch who it is, is someone who is prepared to kill and kill until he has all he wants. He's undoubtedly been successful in the past, which makes it worse. No honest man would have such men as Hansen Bine and Overlin around. They did not ride for Webb . . . we know that now. They ride for whomever it was Webb was fronting. I've got to ride down to Dry Leggett and roust out those wounded men, but you must be careful Ruth . . . this man will stop at nothing."

"But I'm a woman!"

"I don't believe that would matter with this man. He's not like a Western man."

"Be careful, Ward. I just couldn't stand it if anything happened to you."

"You could. You've got the heart as well as the stamina. You've come a long way, Ruth, but you're pioneer stock. There's a rough time in any country, any new, raw country like this, before it can settle down."

As they talked, they wandered out under the trees, and, when they returned to the house, only Baldy was awake.

"Wonder folks wouldn't eat their supper 'stead of standin' around in the dark. A body would think you two wasn't more'n sixteen."

"Shut up, you old squawman," Ward said cheerfully, "and set up the grub. I'm hungry enough to eat even your food."

"Why, Ward," Ruth protested. "How can you talk like that? You know there isn't a better cook west of the Brazos."

Baldy perked up. "See? See there? The boss knows a good cook when she sees one. Why you an' these cowhands around here never knowed what good grub was until I came along. You et sowbelly an' half-baked beans so long you wouldn't recognize real vittles when you see 'em."

A yell interrupted Ward's reply. "Oh, Ward? Ward McQueen!"

Badly Jackson turned impatiently and opened the door.

"What the . . . !"

A bullet struck him as a gun bellowed in the night, and Baldy spun half around, dropping the coffeepot. Three more shots, fast as a man could lever a rifle, punctured the stillness. The light went out as Ward extinguished it with a quick puff and dropped to the floor, pulling Ruth down with him.

As suddenly as it had begun, it ended. In the stillness that followed they heard a hoarse gasping from Baldy. Outside, all was dark and silent except for the pound of hoofs receding in the distance.

As he turned to relight the lamp, there was another shot, this from down the trail where the rider had gone. Glancing out, Ward saw a flare of fire against the woods.

"Take care of Baldy!" he said, and went out fast.

He grabbed a horse from the corral, slipped on a halter, and went down the trail riding bareback. As he drew near the fire, he heard pounding hoofs behind him and slowed up, lifting a hand.

Suddenly he saw a huge man standing in the center of the trail, both hands uplifted so there would be no mistakes.

"McQueen! it's me! I got him!" the man shouted. It was Flagg Warneke.

McQueen swung down, as did Kim Sartain, who had ridden up behind him. A huge pile of grass, dry as tinder, lay in the center of the road, going up in flames. Nearby lay a rider. He was breathing, but there was blood on his shirtfront and blood on the ground.

Warneke said: "I was ridin' to begin work tomorrow and I heard this *hombre* yell, heard the shot, so I threw off my bronc', grabbed an armful of this hay McCracken had cut, and throwed it into the road. As this gent came ridin', I dropped a match into the hay. He tried to shoot me, but this here ol' Spencer is quick. He took a fifty-six right in the chest."

It was the sallow-faced rider Ward had seen before, one of those who had ridden in the posse. "Want to talk?" he asked.

"Go to the devil! Wouldn't if I could!"

"What's that mean? Why couldn't you talk?"

The man raised himself to one elbow, coughing.

"Paid me from a holler tree," he said. "I seen nobody. Webb, he told me where I'd get paid an' how I'd . . . how I'd get word."

The man coughed again and blood trickled over his unshaved chin.

"Maybe it was a woman," he spoke clearly, suddenly. Then his supporting arm seemed to go slack and he fell back, his head striking the ground with a thump. The man was dead.

"A woman?" Ward muttered. "Impossible."

Warneke shook his head. "Maybe . . . I ain't so sure. Could be anybody."

VIII

When the sun was high over the meadows, Ward McQueen was riding beside Ruth Kermitt near a *ciénaga*, following a creek toward Spur Lake. They had left the ranch after daybreak and had skirted some of the finest grazing land in that part of the country. Some areas that to the uninitiated might have seemed too dry she knew would support and fatten cattle. Much seemingly dry brush was good fodder.

"By the way," Ruth inquired, "have you ever heard of a young man, a very handsome young man named Strahan? He spells it with an H but they call him Strann. When I was in Holbrook, there was a Pinkerton man there who was inquiring about this man. He is badly wanted, quite a large reward offered. He held up a Santa Fe train, killing a messenger and a passenger. That was about four months ago. Before that he had been seen around this part of the country, as well as in Santa Fe. Apparently he wrecked another train, killing and injuring passengers. Each time he got away he seemed headed for this part of the country."

"Never heard of him," Ward admitted, "but we're newcomers."

"The Pinkerton man said he was a dead shot with either rifle or pistol, and dangerous. They trailed him to Alma once, and lost him again on the Gila, southeast of here."

They rode on, Ward pointing out landmarks that bordered the ranch. "The Firebox has the best range around," he explained. "The Spur Lake country, all the valley of Centerfire, and over east past the Dry Lakes to Apache Creek. There's timber, with plenty of shade for the hot months, and most of our range has natural boundaries that prevent stock from straying."

"What about this trouble you're having, Ward? Will it be over soon or hanging over our heads for months?"

"It won't hang on. We're going to have a showdown. I'm taking some of the boys, and we're going to round up some of the troublemakers. I'm just sorry that Baldy is laid up. He knows this country better than any of us."

"You'll have trouble leaving him behind, Ward. That was only a flesh wound, even though he lost blood. It was more shock than anything else."

They turned their horses homeward. Ward looked at the wide, beautiful country beyond Centerfire as they topped the ridge. "All this is yours, Ruth. You're no wife for a cowhand now."

"Don't start that. We've been over it before. Who made it all possible for me? If you had not come along when you did, I'd have nothing. Just nothing at all. And if my brother had not been killed, he could not have handled this. Not as you have. He was a fine boy, and no girl ever had a better brother, but he wasn't the cattleman you are.

"And it isn't only that, Ward. You've worked long and you've built my ranch into something worthwhile. At least twice you've protected me when I was about to do something foolish. By rights half of it should belong to you, anyway."

"Maybe what I should do is leave and start a brand of my own. Then I could come back with something behind me."

"How long would that take, Ward?" She put her hand over his on the pommel. "Please, darling, don't even think about it. The thought of you leaving makes me turn cold all over. I have depended on you, Ward, and you've never failed me."

They rode on in silence. A wild turkey flew up, and then vanished in the brush. Ahead of them two deer, feeding early, jumped off into the tall grass and disappeared along the stream.

"Don't you understand? I'm trying to see this your way. You've told me what has to be done and I'm leaving it up to you. I'm not going to interfere. I'm a woman, Ward, and I can't bear to think of you being hurt. Or any of the other boys, for that matter. I'm even more afraid of how all this killing will affect you. I couldn't stand it if you became hard and callous."

"I know what you mean but there's no need to worry about that now. Once, long ago, maybe. Every time I ride into trouble I hate it, but a man must live, and there are those who will ride rough-shod over everybody, given a chance. Unfortunately force is the only way some people understand."

When they dismounted at the cabin, she said: "Then you're riding out tomorrow?"

"Yes."

"Then good luck." She turned quickly and went into the house.

Ward stared after her, feeling suddenly alone and lost. Yet he knew there was no need for it. This was his woman, and they both understood that. She had come with a considerable investment, but with too little practical knowledge of range or cattle. With his hands, his savvy, and his gun he had built most of what she now possessed.

Under his guidance she had bought cattle in Texas, fattened them on the trail north, sold enough in Kansas to pay back her investment, and driven the remainder farther west. Now she controlled extensive range in several states. Alone she never could have done it, nor could Kim, one of the best men with a gun whoever walked, have had the judgment to handle a ranch, and he would have been the first to side-step the responsibility.

Kim came down now. "Tomorrow, Ward?"

"Bring plenty of ammunition, both rifle and pistol. I'll want you, Bud Fox, Shorty Jones, and. . . ."

"Baldy? Boss, if you don't take him, it'll kill him. Or you'll have to hog-tie him to his bunk, and I'm damned if I'd help you. That ol' catamount's a-rarin' to go, an' he's already scared you're plannin' to leave him behind."

"Think he can stand the ride?"

Kim snorted. "Why, that ol' devil will be sittin' a saddle when you an' me are pushin' up daisies. He's tougher'n rawhide an' whalebone."

Daylight came again as the sun chinned itself on the Continental Divide, peering over the heights of the Frisco Mountains and across the Frisco River. In the bottom of the Box, still deep in shadow, rode a small cavalcade of horsemen. In the lead, his battered old hat tugged down to cover his bald spot from the sun, rode Baldy Jackson.

Behind him, with no talking, rode McQueen, Sartain, Fox, and Jones. They rode with awareness, knowing trouble might explode at any moment. Each man knew what he faced on this day, and, once begun, there'd be no stopping. It was war now, a war without flags or drums, a grim war to the death.

For some reason Ward found his thoughts returning time and again to Ruth's account of the Pinkerton who was trailing the handsome killer named Strahan. It was a name he could not remember having heard.

He questioned Baldy. "Strahan? Never heard of a youngster by that name, but there was some folks lived hereabouts some years back named that. A bloody mean outfit, too. Four brothers of them. One was a shorty, a slim, little man but mean as pizen. The others were big men. The oldest one got hisself shot by one o' them Lincoln County gunfighters. Jesse Evans it was, or some friend of his.

"Two of the others, or maybe it was only one of them, got themselves hung by a posse somewhere in Colorado. If this here Strahan is one o' them, watch yourselves because he'd be a bad one."

Their route kept the ridge of the Friscos on their left, and, when they stopped at Baldy's uplifted hand, they were on the edge of a pine-covered basin in the hills.

Ward turned in his saddle and said: "This here's Heifer Basin. It's two miles straight ahead to Dry Leggett. I figure we should take a rest, check our guns, and get set for trouble. If Hansen Bine is down there, this will be war."

Dismounting, they led their horses into the trees. Baldy located a spring he knew, and they sat down beside it. McQueen checked his guns, and then slid them back into their holsters. He rarely had to think of reloading, for it was something he did automatically whenever he used a gun.

"Mighty nice up here," Kim commented. "I always did like high country."

"That's what I like about cowboyin'," Shorty Jones commented. "It's the country you do it in."

"You ever rode in west Texas when the dust was blowin'?" Bud wanted to know.

"I have, an' I liked it. I've rid nearly every kind of country you can call to mind."

"Ssh!" Ward McQueen came to his feet in one easy movement. "On your toes. Here they come."

Into the other end of the basin rode a small group of riders. There were six men, and the last one McQueen recognized as Hansen Bine himself.

Kim Sartain moved off to the right. Baldy rolled over behind a tree trunk and slid his Spencer forward. Jones and Fox scattered in the trees to the left of the spring.

McQueen stepped out into the open. "Bine! We're takin' you in! Drop your gun belts!"

Hansen Bine spurred his horse to the front and dropped from the saddle when no more than fifty paces away. "McQueen, is it? If you're takin' me, you got to do it the hard way!"

He went for his gun.

McQueen had expected it, and the flat hard bark of his pistol was a full beat before Bine's. The bullet struck Bine as his gun was coming up and he twisted sharply with the impact. Ward walked closer, his gun poised. Around him and behind him he heard the roar of guns, and, as Bine fought to bring his gun level, McQueen shot again.

Bine fell, dug his fingers into the turf, heaved himself, trying to rise, and then fell and lay quietly.

Ward looked around to find only empty saddles and one man standing, his left hand high, his right in a sling. "Your name?"

"Bemis." The man's face was pale with shock, but he was not afraid. "I did no shooting. Never was no good with my left hand."

"All right, Bemis. You've been trailing with a pack of coyotes, but, if you talk, you can beat a rope. Who pays you?"

"Bine paid me. Where he got it, I don't know." His eyes sought McQueen's. "You won't believe me but I been wantin' out of this ever since the McCracken shootin'. That was a game kid."

"You helped kill him," McQueen replied coldly. "Who else was in it? Who ran that show?"

"Somebody I'd not seen around before. Young, slight build, but a ring-tailed terror with a gun. He came in with Overlin. Sort of blondish. I never did see him close up. None of us did, 'cept Overlin." Bemis paused again. "Said his name was Strahan."

That name again. The Pinkerton man had been right. Such a man was in this country, hiding out or whatever. Could it be he who was behind this? That did not seem logical. Strahan by all accounts was a hold-up man, gunfighter, whatever, not a cattleman or a cautious planner.

"You goin' to hang me?" Bemis demanded. "If you are, get on with it. I don't like waitin' around."

McQueen turned his eyes on Bemis, and the young cowhand stared back boldly. He was a tough young man, but old in the hard ways of Western life.

"You'll hang, all right. If not now, eventually. That's the road you've taken. But as far as I'm concerned, that's up to the law. Get on your horse."

The others were mounted, and Bine was lying across a saddle. Kim looked apologetic. "He's the only one, boss. The rest of them lit out like who flung the chuck. I think we winged a couple here or there, but they left like their tails was afire."

Kim Sartain looked at Bemis. "Dead or gone, all but this one. Maybe on the way in . . . you know, boss, it's easier to pack a dead man than a live one."

Bemis looked from Sartain to McQueen and back. "Now, see here," he said nervously. "I said I didn't know who did the payin', but I ain't blind. Bine an'

Overlin, they used to see somebody, or meet somebody, in the Emporium. There or the Bat Cave. They used to go to both places."

"So do half the men in the county," McQueen said. "I've been in both places myself." He paused. "How about Strahan?"

"Never seen him before . . . or since."

"Put him on a horse and tie him," McQueen said. "Well give him to Foster."

Ward led the way toward Pelona. There trouble awaited, he knew, and secretly he hoped Foster would be out of town. He wanted no trouble with the old lawman. Foster was a good man in his own way, trying to steer a difficult course in a county where too many men were ready to shoot. Foster was a typical Western sheriff, more successful in rounding up rustlers, horse thieves, and casual outlaws than in dealing with an enemy cunning as a prairie wolf and heartless as a lynx.

They rode swiftly down the cañon to the Tularosa, and then across Polk Mesa to Squirrel Springs Cañon. It was hard riding, and the day was drawing to a close when they reached the plains and cut across toward Pelona. They had ridden far and fast, and both men and horses were done in when they walked their horses up the dusty street to the jail.

Foster came to the door to greet them, glancing from McQueen to Bemis.

"What's the matter with him?"

"He rode with the crowd that killed Jimmy McCracken. Jimmy gave him the bad arm. I've brought him in for trial."

"Who led 'em?" Foster demanded of Bemis.

Bemis hesitated, obviously worried. He glanced around to see who might overhear. "Strahan," he said then. "Bine was in it, too."

Foster's features seemed to age as they watched. For the first time he looked his years.

"Bring him in," Foster said. "Then I'll go after Bine."

"No need to." McQueen jerked his head. "His body's right back there. Look," he added, "we've started a clean-up. We'll finish it."

"You're forgettin' something, McQueen! I'm the law. It's my job."

"Hold your horses, Sheriff. You are the law, but Bine is dead. The boys who were with him are on the run, except for Bemis, and we're turning him over to you. Anybody else who will come willing, we'll bring to you."

"You ain't the law," Foster replied.

"Then make us the law. Deputize us. You can't do it alone, so let us help."

"Makes me look like a quitter."

"Nothing of the kind. Every lawman I know uses deputies, time to time, and I'm asking for the job."

"All right," Foster replied reluctantly. "You brought Bemis in when you could have hung him. I guess you aim to do right."

Outside the sheriff's office, Baldy waited for McQueen. "You name it," he said, as McQueen emerged. "What's next?"

"Fox, you and Shorty get down to the Emporium. If Hutch comes out, one of you follow him.

Let anybody go in who wants to, but watch him."
He turned to Jackson. "Baldy, you get across the
street. Just loaf around, but watch that other store."

"Watch that female? What d'you take me for?
You tryin' to sidetrack me out of this scrap?"

"Get going and do what you're told. Kim, you
come with me. We're going to the Bat Cave."

Foster stared after them, and then walked back
into his office. Bemis stood inside the bars of his
cell door. "I'm gettin' old, Bemis," Foster said. "Let-
tin' another man do my job."

He sat down in his swivel chair. He was scared—
he admitted it to himself. Scared not of guns or
violence but of what he might find. Slowly the fog
had been clearing, and the things he had been
avoiding could no longer be avoided. It was better
to let McQueen handle it, much better.

"Leave it to McQueen," Bemis was saying. "Mc-
Queen was right, and he's square." He clutched
the bars. "Believe me, Sheriff, I never thought I'd
be glad to be in jail, but I am. Before this day is over
men will die. Foster, you should have seen Mc-
Queen when he killed Bine. I never would have
believed anybody could beat Bine so bad. Bine
slapped leather and died, just like that."

"But there's Overlin," Foster said.

"Yeah, that will be somethin' to see. McQueen
an' Overlin." Suddenly Bemis exclaimed: "Foster!
I forgot to tell them about Ren Oliver!"

"Oliver? Don't tell me he's involved?"

"Involved? He might be the ringleader, the boss
man. And he packs a sneak gun. A stingy gun.

Whilst you're expecting him to move for the gun you can see, he kills you with the other one."

Foster was on his feet. "Thanks, Bemis. We'll remember that when you're up for trial."

As Foster went out of the door, Bemis said: "Maybe, but maybe it's too late."

IX

The Bat Cave was alive and sinning. It was packed at this hour, and all the tables were busy. Behind one of them, seated where he could face the door, was Ren Oliver. His hair was neatly waved back from his brow, his handsome face composed as he dealt the tricky pasteboards with easy, casual skill. Only his eyes seemed alive, missing nothing. In the stable back of the house where he lived was a saddled horse. It was just a little bit of insurance.

At the bar, drinking heavily, was Overlin. Like a huge grizzly he hulked against the bar. The more he drank, the colder and deadlier he became. Someday that might change, and he was aware of it. He thought he would know when that time came, but for the present he was a man to be left strictly alone when drinking. He had been known to go berserk. Left alone, he usually drank the evening away, speaking to no one, bothering no one until finally he went home to sleep it off.

Around him men might push and shove for places at the bar, but they avoided Overlin.

The smoke-laden atmosphere was thick, redolent of cheap perfume, alcohol, and sweaty, unwashed bodies. The night was chill, so the two stoves glowed cherry red. Two bartenders, working swiftly, tried to keep up with the demands of the customers.

Tonight was different, and the bartenders had been the first to sense it. Overlin only occasionally came in, and they were always uncomfortable until he left. It was like serving an old grizzly with a sore tooth. But Overlin was only part of the trouble. The air was tense. They could feel trouble.

The burning of Bear Cañon, the slaying of Chalk Warneke, and the gun battle in Heifer Basin were being talked about, but only in low tones. From time to time, in spite of themselves, their eyes went to Overlin. They were not speculating if he would meet McQueen, but when.

Overlin called for another drink, and the big gunfighter ripped the bottle from the bartender's hand and put it down beside him. The bartender retreated hastily, while somebody started a tear-jerking ballad at the old piano.

The door opened and Ward McQueen stepped in, followed by Kim Sartain.

Kim, lithe as a young panther, moved swiftly to one side, his eyes sweeping the room, picking up Ren Oliver at once, and then Overlin.

Ward McQueen did not stop walking until he was at the bar six feet from Overlin. As the big gunman reached again for the bottle, McQueen knocked it from under his hand.

At the crash of the breaking bottle the room became soundless. Not even the entry of Sheriff Foster was noted, except by Sartain.

"Overlin, I'm acting as deputy sheriff. I want you out of town by noon tomorrow. Ride, keep riding, and don't come back."

"So you're McQueen? And you got Bine? Well, that must have surprised Hans. He always thought he was good. Even thought he was better'n me, but he wasn't. He never saw the day."

McQueen waited. He had not expected the man to leave. This would be a killing for one or the other, but he had to give the man a chance to make it official. Proving that he had had a hand in the murder of Jimmy McCracken would have been difficult at best.

Overlin was different from Bine. It would take a lot of lead to sink that big body.

"Where's Strahan?" McQueen demanded.

Ren Oliver started, and then glanced hastily toward the door. His eyes met those of Kim Sartain, and he knew that to attempt to leave would mean a shoot-out, and he was not ready for that.

"Strahan, is it? Even if you get by me, you'll never get past him. No need to tell you where he is. He'll find you when you least expect it."

Deliberately Overlin turned his eyes away from McQueen, reaching for his glass with his left hand. "Whiskey! Gimme some whiskey!"

"Where is he, Overlin? Where's Strahan?"

The men were ready, McQueen knew. Inside of him, Overlin was poised for the kill. McQueen wanted to startle him, to throw him off balance, to wreck his poise. He took a half step closer. "Tell me, you drunken lobo. Tell me!"

As he spoke, he struck swiftly with his left hand and slapped Overlin across the mouth.

It was a powerful slap and it shocked Overlin. Not since he was a child had anybody dared to strike him, and it shook him as nothing else could have. He uttered a cry of choking rage and went for his gun.

Men dived for cover, falling over splintering chairs, fighting to get out of range or out the door.

McQueen had already stepped back quickly, drawn his gun, and then stepped off to the left as he fired, forcing Overlin to turn toward him. McQueen's first bullet struck an instant before Overlin could fire, and the impact knocked Overlin against the bar, his shot going off into the floor as McQueen fired again.

Overlin faced around, his shirt bloody, one eye gone, and his gun blazed again. McQueen felt himself stagger, shaken as if by a blow, yet without any realization of where the blow had come from.

He fired again, and, not aware of how many shots he had fired, he drew his left-hand gun and pulled a border shift, tossing the guns from hand to hand to have a fully loaded gun in his right.

Across the room behind him, another brief drama played itself out. Ren Oliver had been watching and thought he saw his chance. Under cover of the action, all attention centered on McQueen and Overlin, he would kill McQueen. His sleeve gun dropped into his hand and cut down on McQueen, but the instant the flash of blue steel appeared in his hand, two guns centered on him and fired. Sartain was at the front door and Sheriff Foster on his left

rear. Struck by a triangle of lead, Oliver lunged to
his feet. one hand going to his stomach. In amazement, he stared at his bloody hand and his shattered body. Then he screamed.

In that scream was all the coward's fear of the
death he had brought to so many others. In shocked
amazement he stared from Foster to Sartain, both
holding guns ready for another shot if need be.
Then his legs wilted and he fell, one hand clutching at the falling deck of cards, his blood staining
them. He fell, and the table tipped, cascading chips
and cards over him and into the sawdust around
him.

At the bar, Overlin stood, indomitable spirit still
blazing from his remaining eye. "You . . . ! You . . . !"

As he started to fall, his big hand caught at the
bar's rounded edge and he stared at McQueen,
trying to speak. Then the fingers gave way and he
fell, striking the brass rail and rolling away.

Ward McQueen turned as if from a bad dream,
seeing Kim at the door and Sheriff Foster, gun in
hand, inside the rear door.

Running feet pounded the boardwalk, and the
door slammed open. Guns lifted expectantly.

It was Baldy Jackson, his face white, torn with
emotion. "Ward! Heaven help me! I've killed a
woman! I've killed Sharon Clarity!"

The scattered spectators were suddenly a mob.
"What?" They started for him.

"Hold it!" McQueen's gun came up. "Hear him
out!" Ward McQueen was thumbing shells into
his gun. "All right, Baldy. Show us."

"Before my Maker, Ward, I figured her for

somebody sneakin' to get a shot at me! I seen the gun, plain as day, an' I fired!"

Muttering and angry, the crowd followed. Baldy led the way to an alley behind the store, where they stopped. There lay a still figure in a riding habit. For an instant Ward looked down at that still, strangely attractive face.

Then he bent swiftly, and, as several cried out in protest, he seized Sharon Clarity's red gold hair and jerked.

It came free in his hand, and the head flopped back on the earth, the close-cropped head of a man.

Ward stooped, gripped the neckline, and ripped it away. With the padding removed, all could see the chest of a man, lean, muscular, and hairy.

"Not Sharon Clarity," he said, "but Strahan."

Kim Sartain wheeled and walked swiftly away, McQueen following. As they reached the Emporium, Bud Fox appeared.

"Nobody left here but that girl. She was in there a long time. The old man started out, but we warned him back. He's inside."

Ward McQueen led the way, with Sheriff Foster behind him, then Sartain, Jackson, Fox, and Jones.

Silas Hutch sat at his battered rolltop desk. His lean jaws seemed leaner than ever. He peered at them from eyes that were mean and cruel. "Well? What's this mean? Bargin' in like this?"

"You're under arrest, Hutch, for ordering the killing of Jimmy McCracken and Neal Webb."

Hutch chuckled. "Me? Under arrest? You got a

lot to learn, boy. The law here answers to me. I say who is to be arrested and who is prosecuted. You got no proof of anything. You got no evidence. You're talkin' up the wind, sonny."

Baldy Jackson pushed forward. "Ward, this here's the one I told you about. This is the first time I've had a good look at him. He's Shorty Strahan, the mean one. He's an uncle, maybe, of that one out there who made such a fine-lookin' woman."

"Hutch, you had your killings done for you. All but one. You killed Chalk Warneke." He turned to Foster. "Figure it out for yourself, Sheriff. Remember the position Chalk was in, remember the crowd, and Warneke on a horse. There's only one place that shot could come from . . . that window. And only one man who could have fired it. Him."

Silas Hutch shrank back in his chair. When Foster reached for him, he cringed. "Don't let them hang me," he pleaded.

"You take it from here, Foster," McQueen said. "We can mesure the angle of that bullet and you've got Bemis. He can testify as to the connection between Neal Webb and Hutch as well as that with Chalk. He knows all about it."

Ward McQueen turned toward the door. He was tired, very tired, and all he wanted was rest. Besides, his hip bone was bothering him. He had been aware of it for some time, but only now was it really hurting. He looked down, remembering something hitting him during the battle with Overlin.

His gun belt was somewhat torn and two cartridges dented. A bullet had evidently struck and glanced off, running two perfectly good cartridges and giving him a bad bruise on the hip bone. "Kim," he said, "let's get back to the ranch."

About the Editor

Jon Tuska is the author of numerous books about the American West as well as editor of several short story collections, *Billy the Kid: His Life and Legend* (Greenwood Press, 1994) and *The Western Story: A Chronological Treasury* (University of Nebraska Press, 1995) among them. Together with his wife Vicki Piekarski, Tuska co-founded Golden West Literary Agency that primarily represents authors of Western fiction and Western Americana. They edit and copublish twenty-six titles a year in two prestigious series of new hardcover Western novels and story collections, the Five Star Westerns and the Circle ς Westerns. They also coedited the *Encyclopedia of Frontier and Western Fiction* (McGraw-Hill, 1983), *The Max Brand Companion* (Greenwood Press, 1996), *The Morrow Anthology of Great Western Short Stories* (Morrow, 1997), and *The First Five Star Western Corral* (Five Star Westerns, 2000). Tuska has also edited a series of short novel collections, *Stories of the Golden West*, of which there have been seven volumes.

SHOWDOWN AT JUNIPER PASS

To give his Apache brother Nana a traditional burial, Jake Slade and his other brother Paleto will have to risk the dangerous Sangre De Cristo Mountains in the dead of winter—a risk they're willing to take. But the elements aren't the only thing Slade and Paleto have to fear . . .

Frank Tolliver is gathering men—hired guns—and positioning himself to take control of those mountains. The mountains produce gold, gold that must travel over Juniper Pass on its way to the safety of a Las Vegas bank. And whoever gets in Tolliver's way, whether they're innocent townsfolk or Jake and Paleto, meet with a bad end. But unlike the townsfolk, Jake and Paleto will not bend to Tolliver's will. They will outsmart, outshoot, and outride the gunslingers if that's what it takes to liberate the mountains and honor the memory of their fallen brother.

Kent Conwell

ISBN 13: 978-0-8439-6359-5

✂ ☐ **YES!**

Sign me up for the Leisure Western Book Club and send my FREE BOOKS! If I choose to stay in the club, I will pay only $14.00* each month, a savings of $9.96!

NAME: _____

ADDRESS: _____

TELEPHONE: _____

EMAIL: _____

☐ I want to pay by credit card.

☐ **VISA**   ☐ **MasterCard**   ☐ **DISCOVER**

ACCOUNT #: _____

EXPIRATION DATE: _____

SIGNATURE: _____

Mail this page along with $2.00 shipping and handling to:
Leisure Western Book Club
PO Box 6640
Wayne, PA 19087
Or fax (must include credit card information) to:
610-995-9274

You can also sign up online at **www.dorchesterpub.com**.

*Plus $2.00 for shipping. Offer open to residents of the U.S. and Canada only. Canadian residents please call 1-800-481-9191 for pricing information.

If under 18, a parent or guardian must sign. Terms, prices and conditions subject to change. Subscription subject to acceptance. Dorchester Publishing reserves the right to reject any order or cancel any subscription.